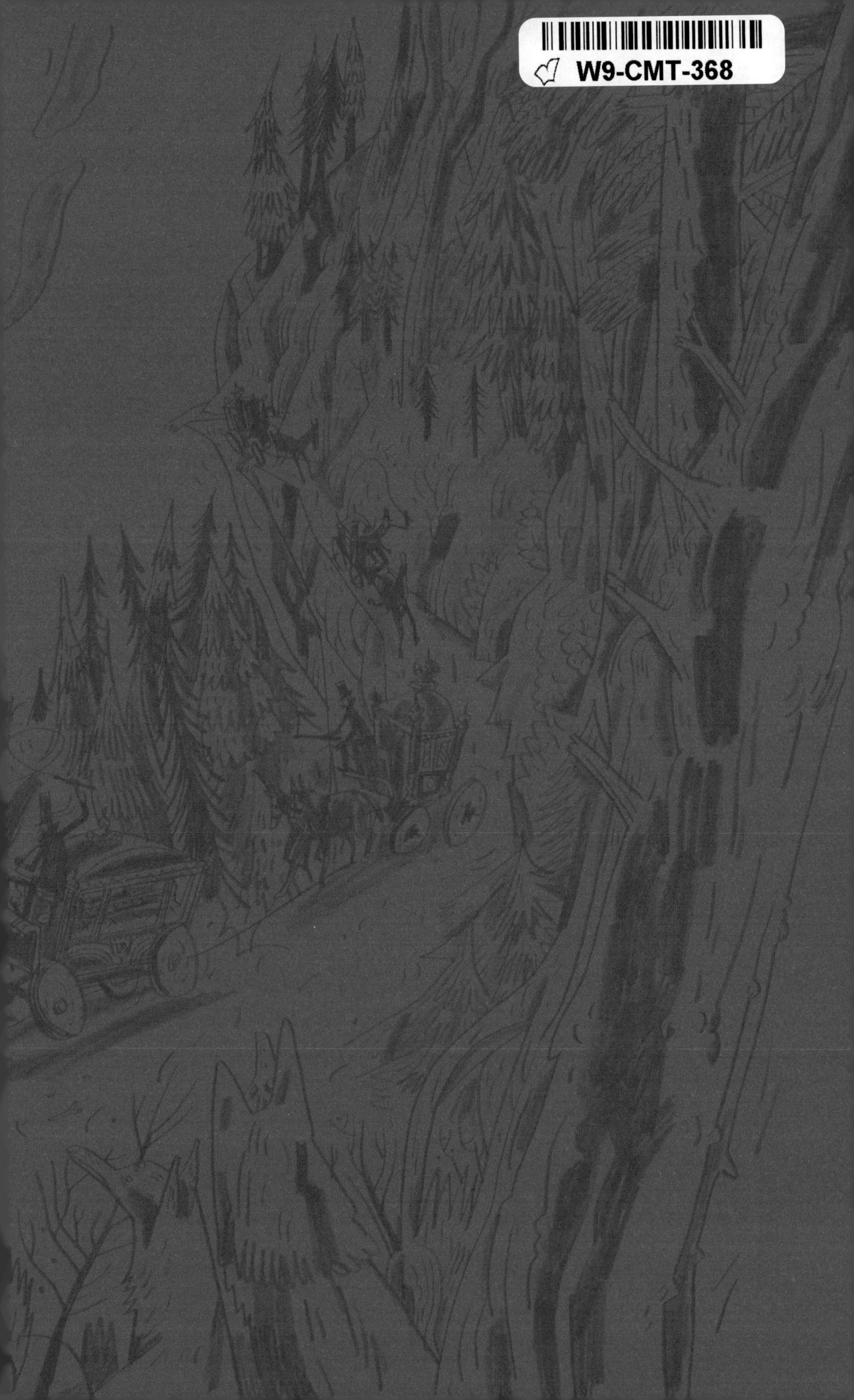

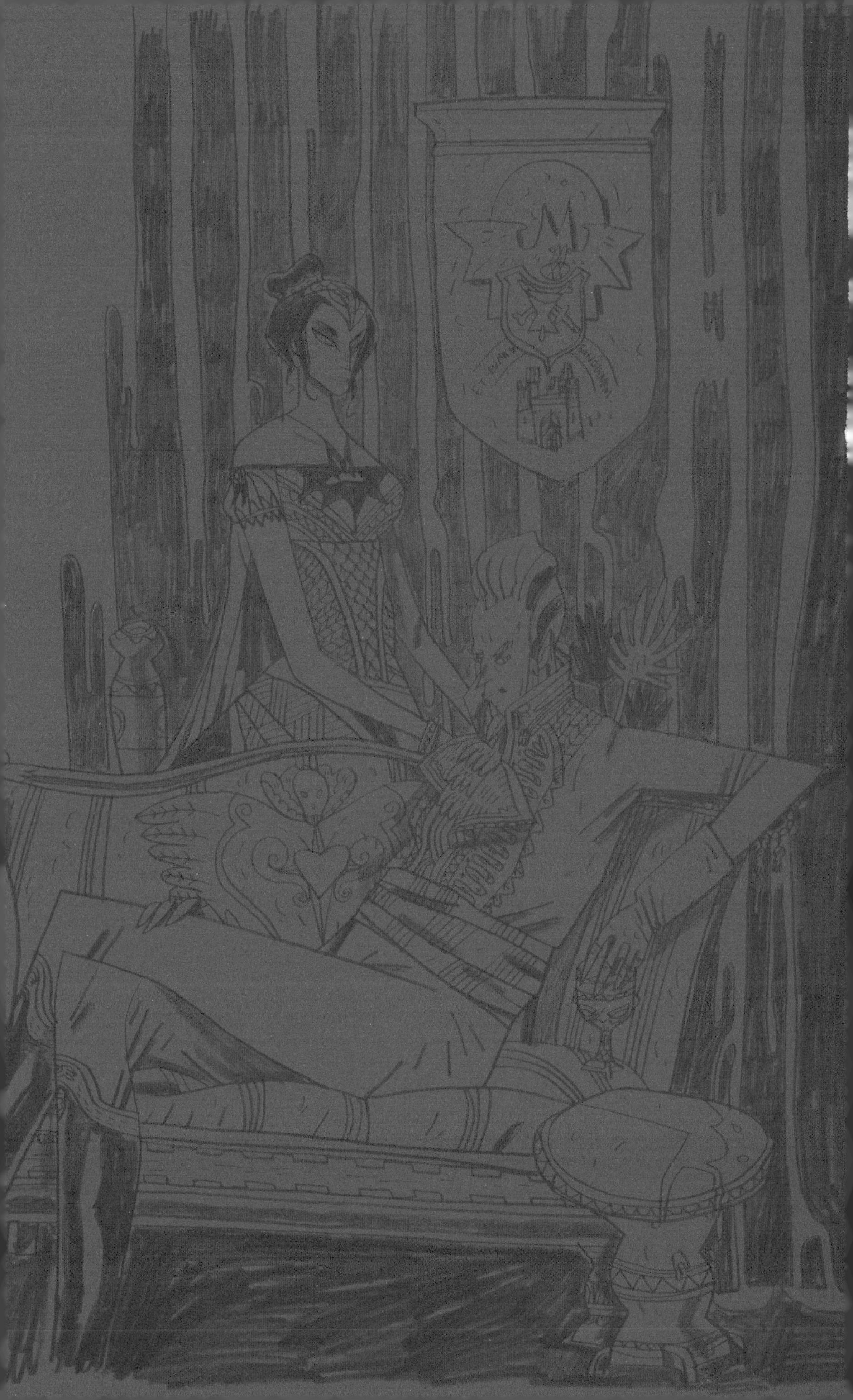

MR. HIGGINS
COMES HOME

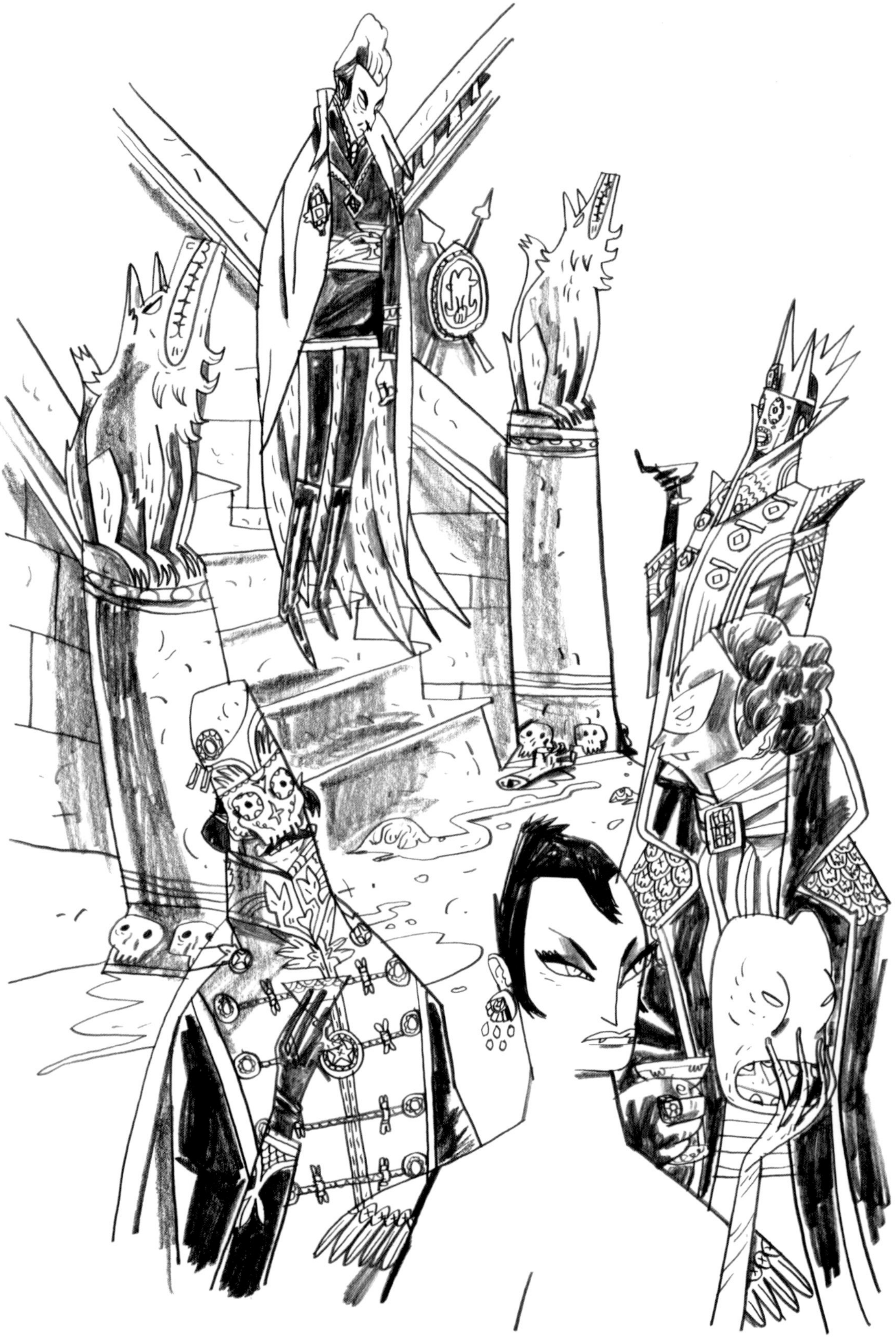

MR. HIGGINS
COMES HOME

Story by
MIKE MIGNOLA

Art by
WARWICK JOHNSON-CADWELL

Letters by
CLEM ROBINS

Cover art by
MIKE MIGNOLA
with **DAVE STEWART**

President and Publisher MIKE RICHARDSON
Editor SCOTT ALLIE
Assistant Editor KATII O'BRIEN
Collection Designer ETHAN KIMBERLING
Digital Art Technician CHRISTINA McKENZIE

DARK HORSE BOOKS

Neil Hankerson *Executive Vice President* Tom Weddle *Chief Financial Officer* Randy Stradley *Vice President of Publishing* Matt Parkinson *Vice President of Marketing* David Scroggy *Vice President of Product Development* Dale LaFountain *Vice President of Information Technology* Cara Niece *Vice President of Production and Scheduling* Nick McWhorter *Vice President of Media Licensing* Mark Bernardi *Vice President of Book Trade and Digital Sales* Ken Lizzi *General Counsel* Dave Marshall *Editor in Chief* Davey Estrada *Editorial Director* Scott Allie *Executive Senior Editor* Chris Warner *Senior Books Editor* Cary Grazzini *Director of Specialty Projects* Lia Ribacchi *Art Director* Vanessa Todd *Director of Print Purchasing* Matt Dryer *Director of Digital Art and Prepress* Sarah Robertson *Director of Product Sales* Michael Gombos *Director of International Publishing and Licensing*

Published by Dark Horse Books
A division of Dark Horse Comics, Inc.
10956 SE Main Street
Milwaukie, OR 97222

Advertising Sales (503) 905-2237
International Licensing (503) 905-2377
Comic Shop Locator Service (888) 266-4226

DarkHorse.com

Facebook.com/DarkHorseComics
Twitter.com/DarkHorseComics

First edition: October 2017
ISBN 978-1-50670-466-1

MR. HIGGINS COMES HOME

10 9 8 7 6 5 4 3 2 1
Printed in China

Library of Congress Cataloging-in-Publication Data

Names: Mignola, Michael, author, artist. | Johnson-Cadwell, Warwick, artist.
| Stewart, Dave, artist.
Title: Mr. Higgins comes home / story by Mike Mignola ; art by Warwick
Johnson-Cadwell ; letters by Clem Robins ; cover art by Mike Mignola with
Dave Stewart.
Other titles: Mister Higgins comes home
Description: First edition. | Milwaukie, OR : Dark Horse Books, 2017.
Identifiers: LCCN 2017020492 | ISBN 9781506704661 (hardback)
Subjects: LCSH: Graphic novels. | BISAC: COMICS & GRAPHIC NOVELS / Horror. |
COMICS & GRAPHIC NOVELS / Fantasy. | FICTION / Occult & Supernatural.
Classification: LCC PN6727.M53 M7 2017 | DDC 741.5/973--dc23
LC record available at https://lccn.loc.gov/2017020492

This one owes everything to those great old Hammer vampire films (all those Draculas, Brides of Dracula, Twins of Evil, Captain Kronos, etc.), and, especially, to my all-time favorite vampire film, Polanski's The Fearless Vampire Killers.
—MIKE MIGNOLA

For the movie monsters that kept me up at night as a nipper (drawing them rather than worrying about them), and also for my family, who I may worry about but seldom draw.
—WARWICK JOHNSON-CADWELL

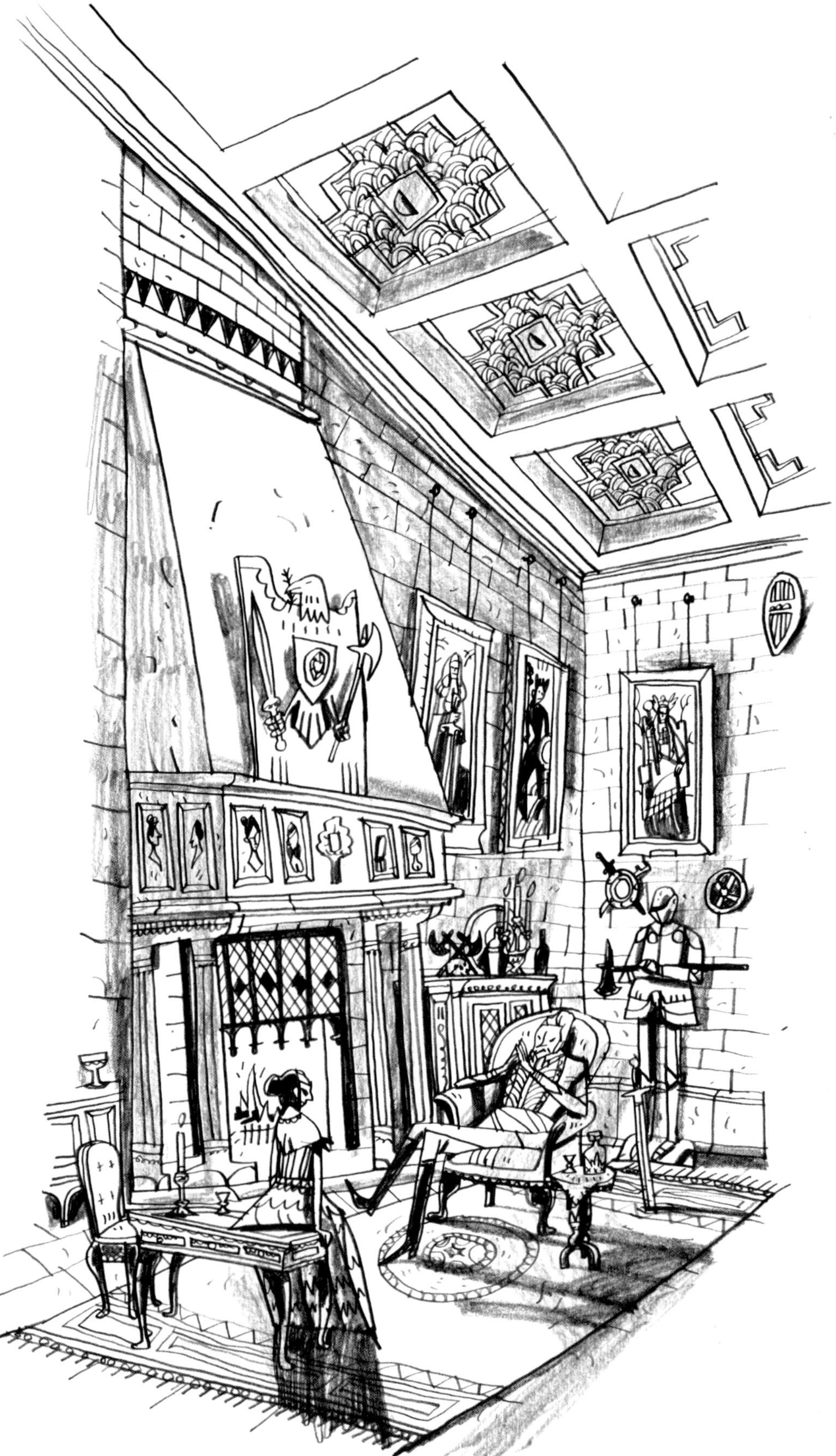

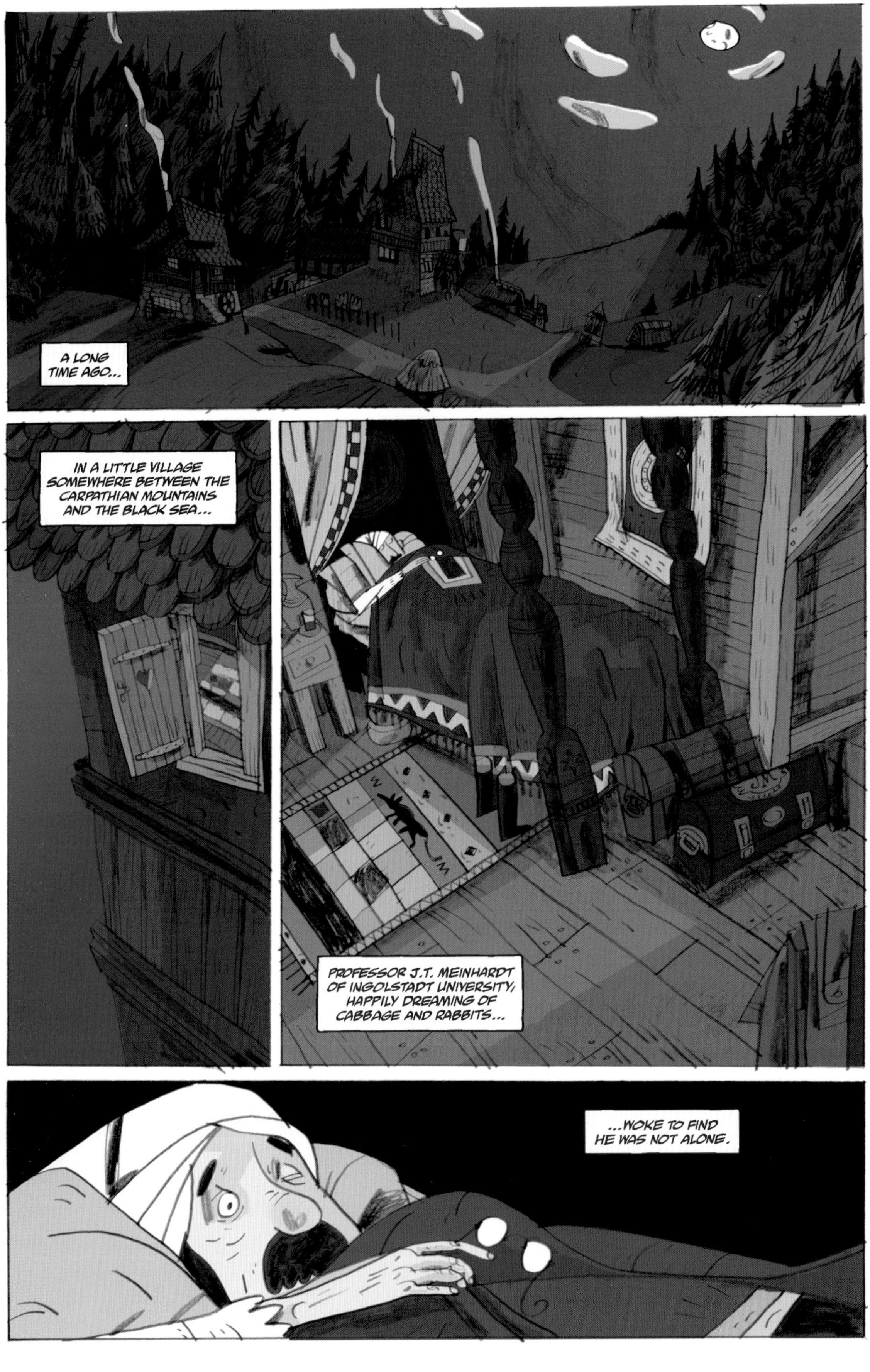
A LONG TIME AGO...
IN A LITTLE VILLAGE SOMEWHERE BETWEEN THE CARPATHIAN MOUNTAINS AND THE BLACK SEA...
PROFESSOR J.T. MEINHARDT OF INGOLSTADT UNIVERSITY, HAPPILY DREAMING OF CABBAGE AND RABBITS...
...WOKE TO FIND HE WAS NOT ALONE.

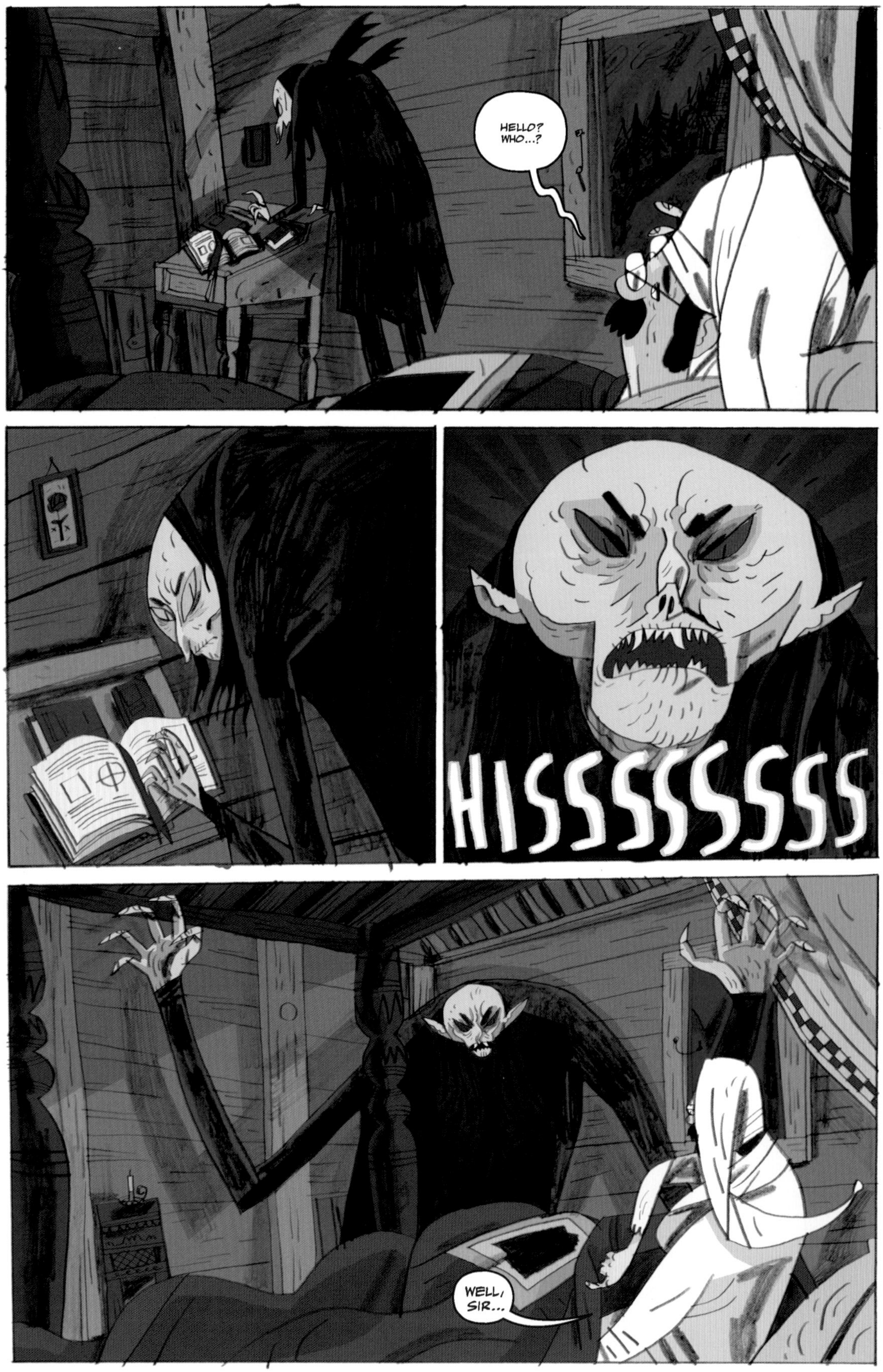
HELLO? WHO...?
HISSSSSSSSS
WELL, SIR...

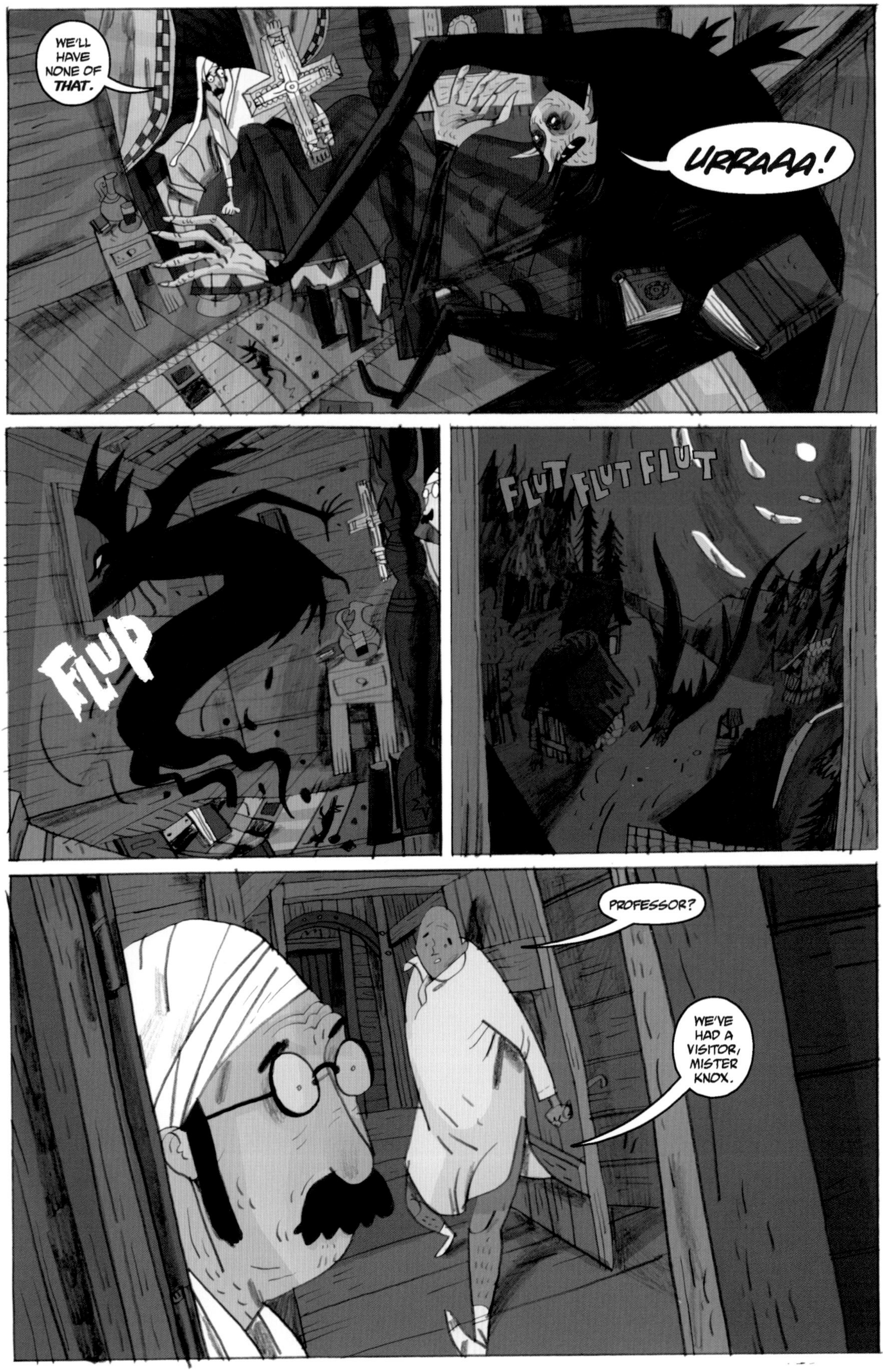
WE'LL HAVE NONE OF THAT.
URRAAA!
FLUP
FLUT FLUT FLUT
PROFESSOR?
WE'VE HAD A VISITOR, MISTER KNOX.

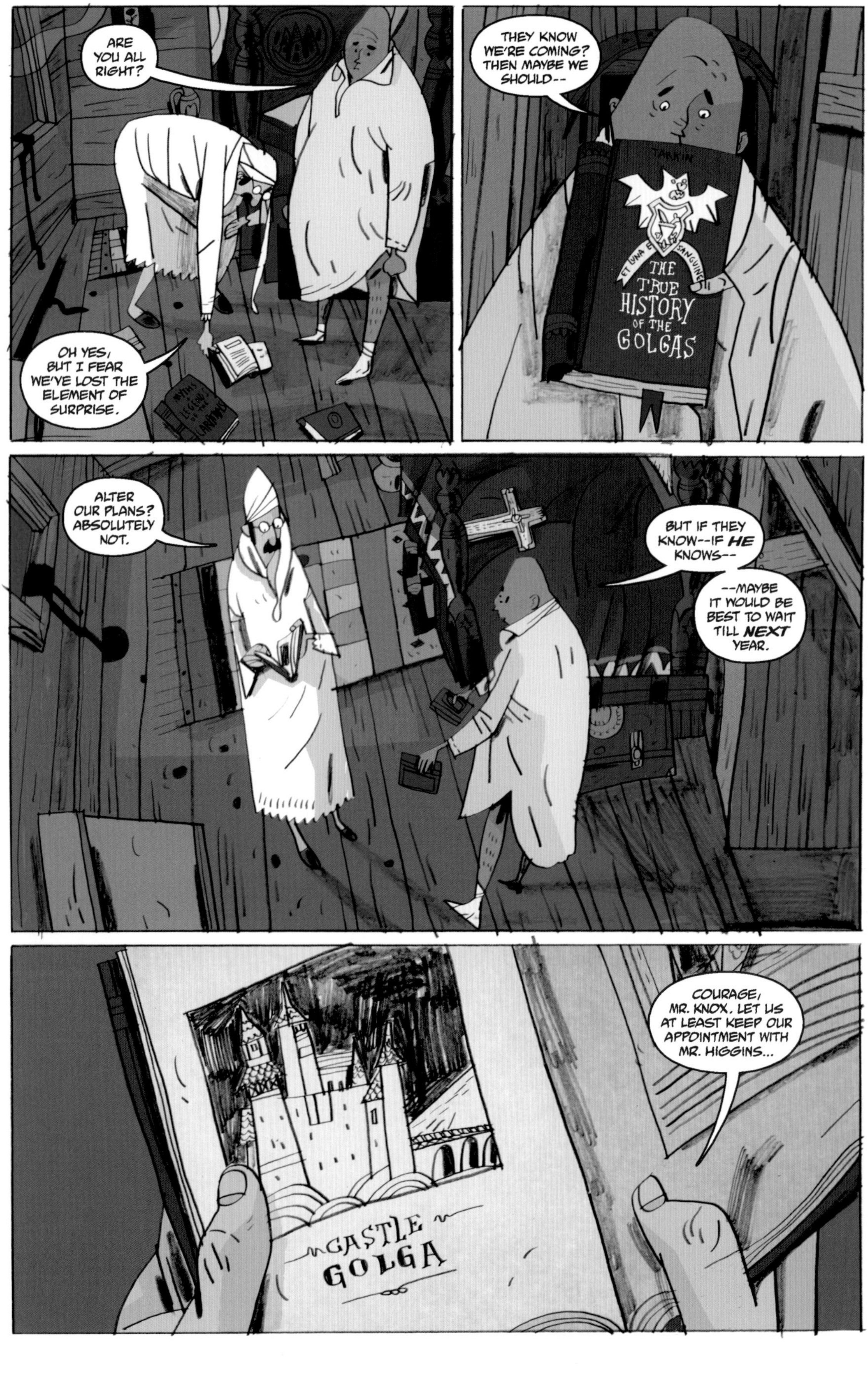
ARE YOU ALL RIGHT?
OH YES, BUT I FEAR WE'VE LOST THE ELEMENT OF SURPRISE.
THEY KNOW WE'RE COMING? THEN MAYBE WE SHOULD--
ET LUNA E SANGUINE
THE TRUE HISTORY OF THE GOLGAS
ALTER OUR PLANS? ABSOLUTELY NOT.
BUT IF THEY KNOW--IF **HE** KNOWS--
--MAYBE IT WOULD BE BEST TO WAIT TILL **NEXT** YEAR.
COURAGE, MR. KNOX. LET US AT LEAST KEEP OUR APPOINTMENT WITH MR. HIGGINS...
CASTLE GOLGA

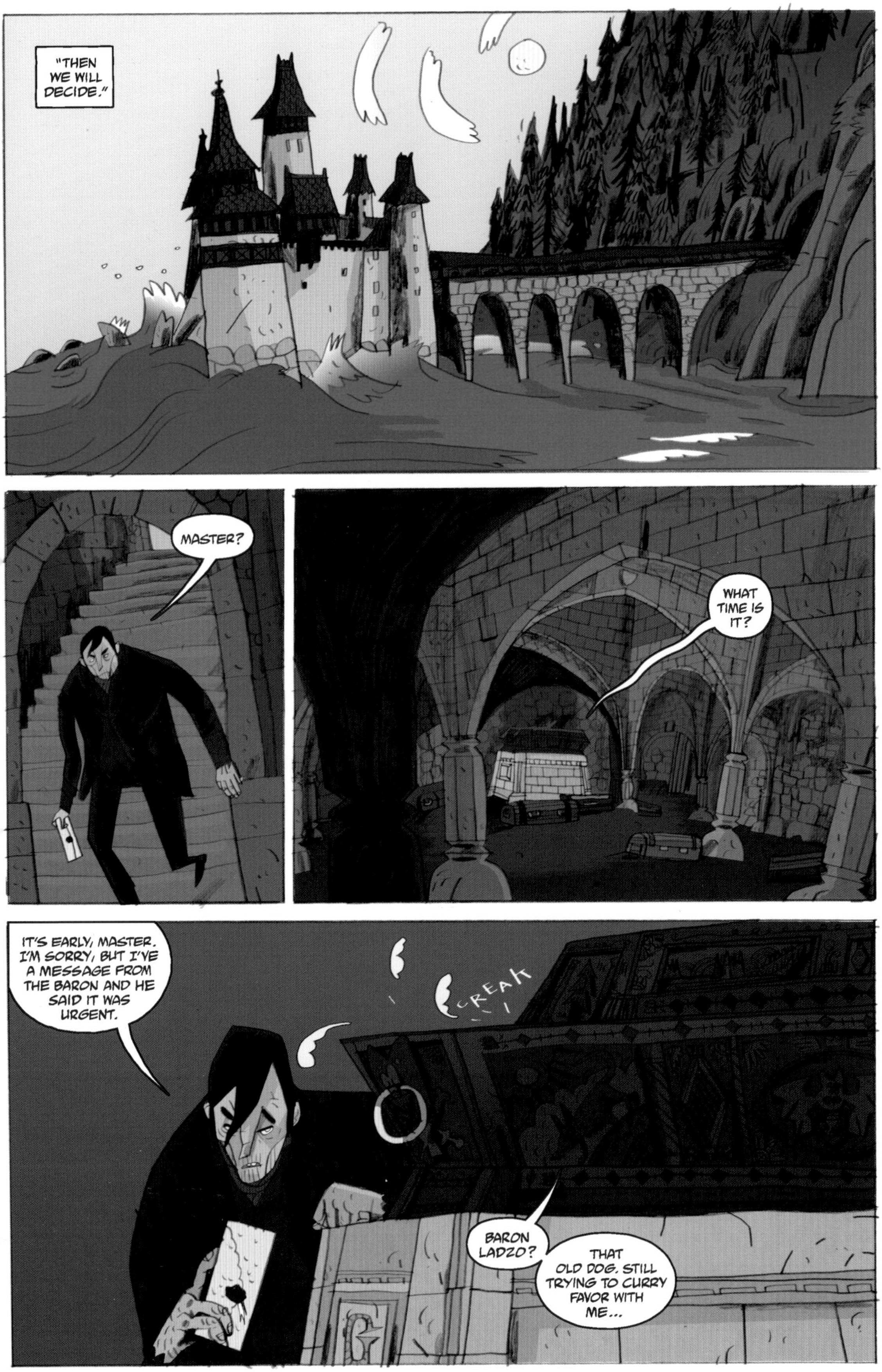
"THEN WE WILL DECIDE."
MASTER?
WHAT TIME IS IT?
IT'S EARLY, MASTER. I'M SORRY, BUT I'VE A MESSAGE FROM THE BARON AND HE SAID IT WAS URGENT.
CREAK
BARON LADZO?
THAT OLD DOG. STILL TRYING TO CURRY FAVOR WITH ME...

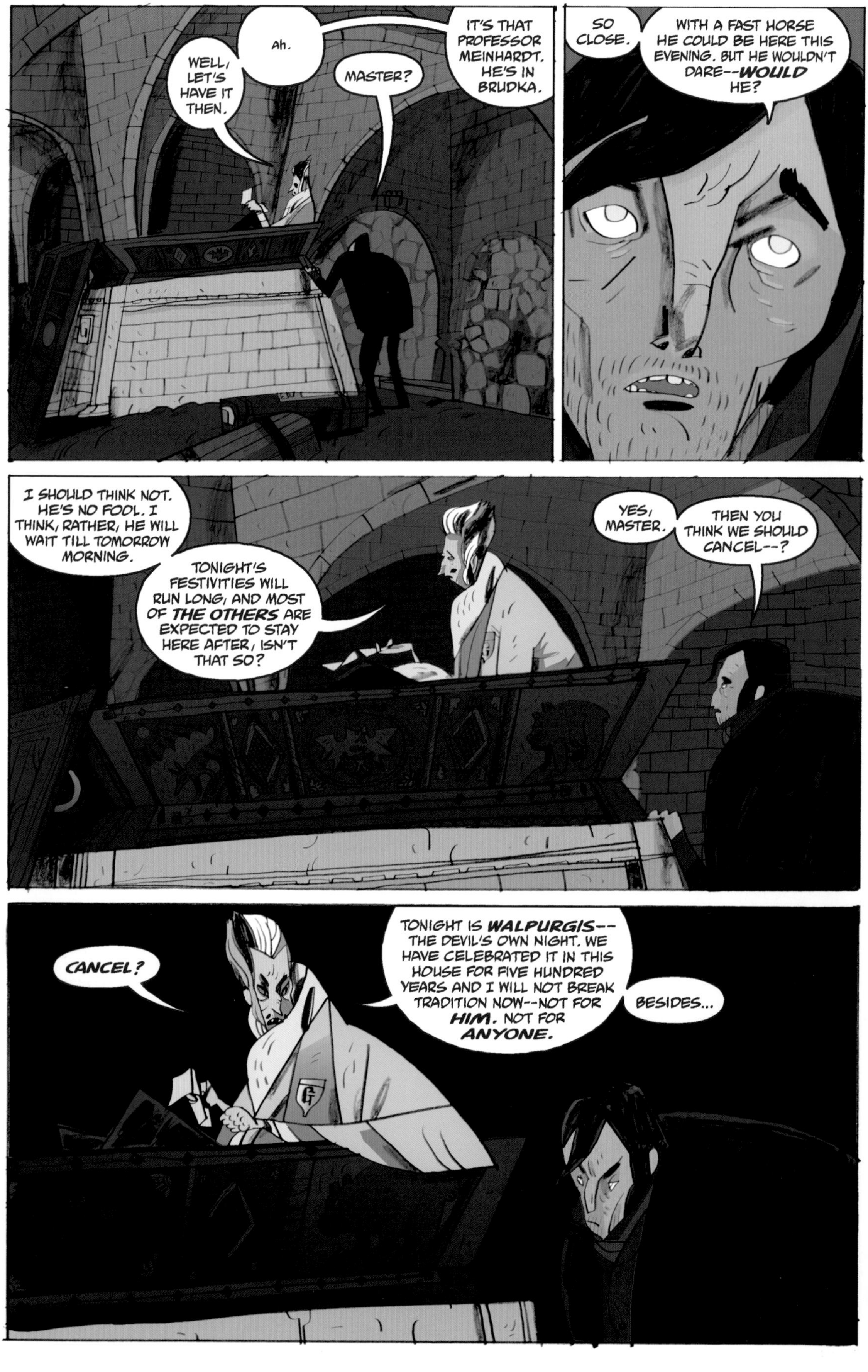
IT'S THAT PROFESSOR MEINHARDT. HE'S IN BRUDKA.
MASTER?
Ah.
WELL, LET'S HAVE IT THEN.
SO CLOSE.
WITH A FAST HORSE HE COULD BE HERE THIS EVENING. BUT HE WOULDN'T DARE--WOULD HE?
I SHOULD THINK NOT. HE'S NO FOOL. I THINK, RATHER, HE WILL WAIT TILL TOMORROW MORNING.
TONIGHT'S FESTIVITIES WILL RUN LONG, AND MOST OF THE OTHERS ARE EXPECTED TO STAY HERE AFTER, ISN'T THAT SO?
YES, MASTER.
THEN YOU THINK WE SHOULD CANCEL--?
CANCEL?
TONIGHT IS WALPURGIS-- THE DEVIL'S OWN NIGHT. WE HAVE CELEBRATED IT IN THIS HOUSE FOR FIVE HUNDRED YEARS AND I WILL NOT BREAK TRADITION NOW--NOT FOR HIM. NOT FOR ANYONE.
BESIDES...

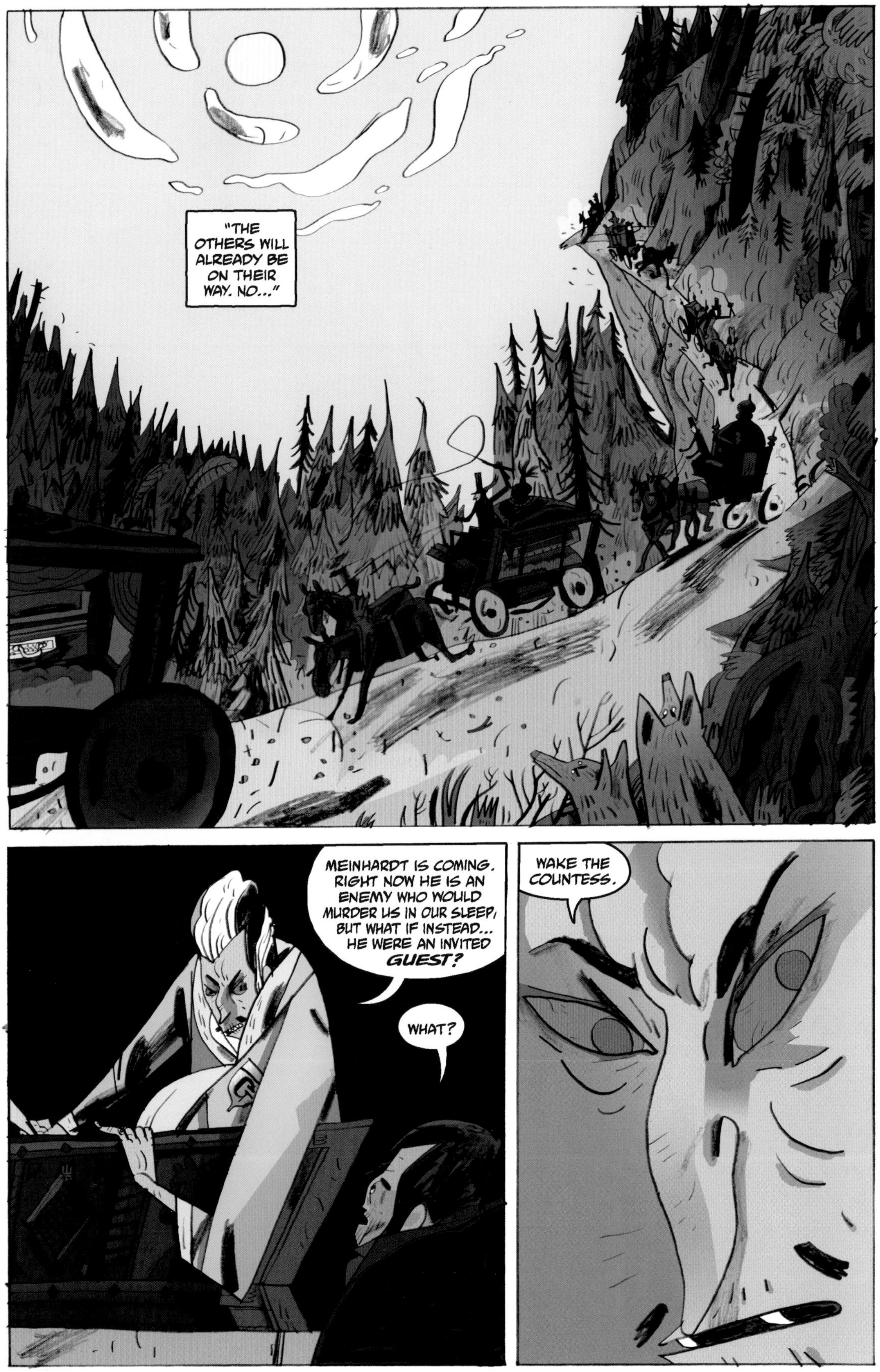
"THE OTHERS WILL ALREADY BE ON THEIR WAY. NO..."
MEINHARDT IS COMING. RIGHT NOW HE IS AN ENEMY WHO WOULD MURDER US IN OUR SLEEP, BUT WHAT IF INSTEAD... HE WERE AN INVITED GUEST?
WHAT?
WAKE THE COUNTESS.

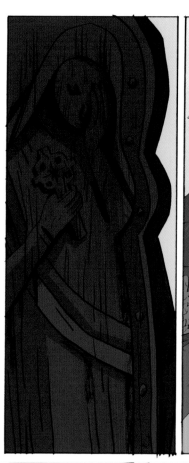

I WROTE YOU LAST MONTH--

OF COURSE, PROFESSOR. REGARDING OUR POOR MR. HIGGINS...

HE'S BEEN WITH US FOR YEARS NOW, SINCE HE WAS CAUGHT ATTACKING ALL THOSE SHEEP.

SHEEP?

APPARENTLY HE WAS QUITE THE SAVAGE. IMPOSSIBLE TO BELIEVE NOW-- HE'S REALLY SUCH A *DEAR* MAN. AND SO SAD.

YOU'LL SEE FOR YOUR-SELF.

MR. HIGGINS, YOU HAVE VISITORS.

REMEMBER, I TOLD YOU...?

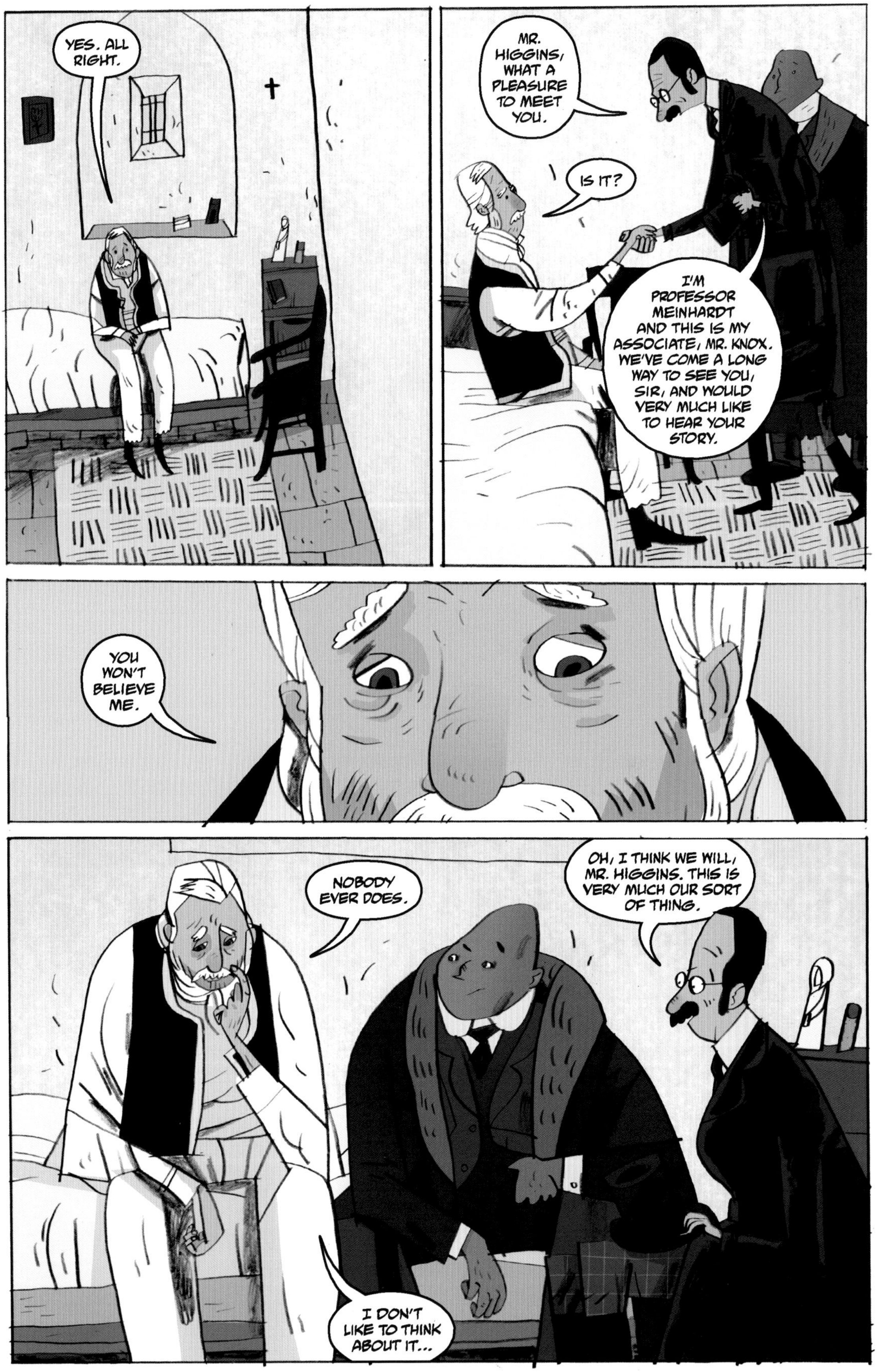
YES. ALL RIGHT.
MR. HIGGINS, WHAT A PLEASURE TO MEET YOU.
IS IT?
I'M PROFESSOR MEINHARDT AND THIS IS MY ASSOCIATE, MR. KNOX. WE'VE COME A LONG WAY TO SEE YOU, SIR, AND WOULD VERY MUCH LIKE TO HEAR YOUR STORY.
YOU WON'T BELIEVE ME.
NOBODY EVER DOES.
OH, I THINK WE WILL, MR. HIGGINS. THIS IS VERY MUCH OUR SORT OF THING.
I DON'T LIKE TO THINK ABOUT IT...

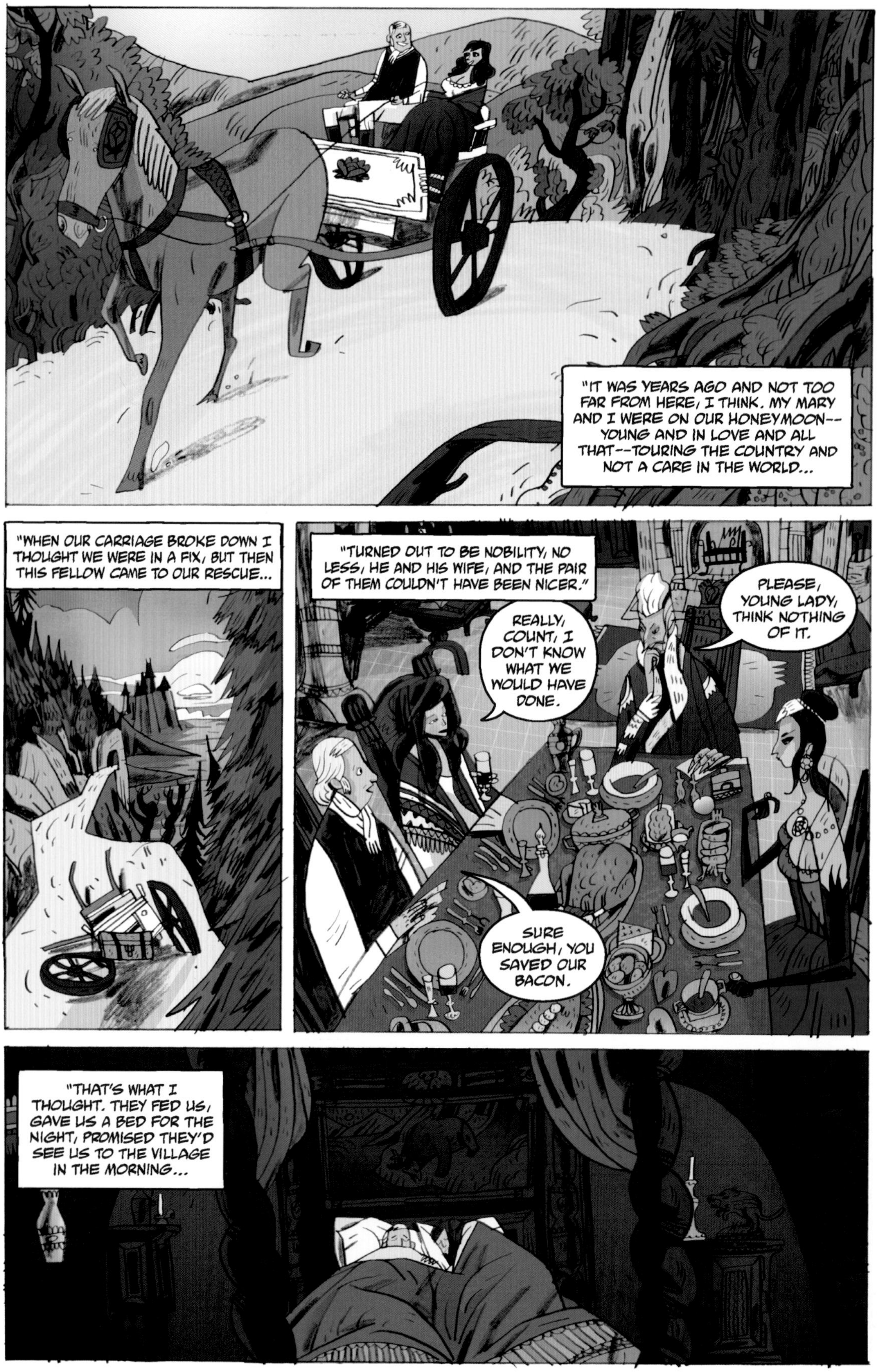
"IT WAS YEARS AGO AND NOT TOO FAR FROM HERE, I THINK. MY MARY AND I WERE ON OUR HONEYMOON-- YOUNG AND IN LOVE AND ALL THAT--TOURING THE COUNTRY AND NOT A CARE IN THE WORLD...
"WHEN OUR CARRIAGE BROKE DOWN I THOUGHT WE WERE IN A FIX, BUT THEN THIS FELLOW CAME TO OUR RESCUE...
"TURNED OUT TO BE NOBILITY, NO LESS, HE AND HIS WIFE, AND THE PAIR OF THEM COULDN'T HAVE BEEN NICER."
REALLY, COUNT, I DON'T KNOW WHAT WE WOULD HAVE DONE.
PLEASE, YOUNG LADY, THINK NOTHING OF IT.
SURE ENOUGH, YOU SAVED OUR BACON.
"THAT'S WHAT I THOUGHT. THEY FED US, GAVE US A BED FOR THE NIGHT, PROMISED THEY'D SEE US TO THE VILLAGE IN THE MORNING...

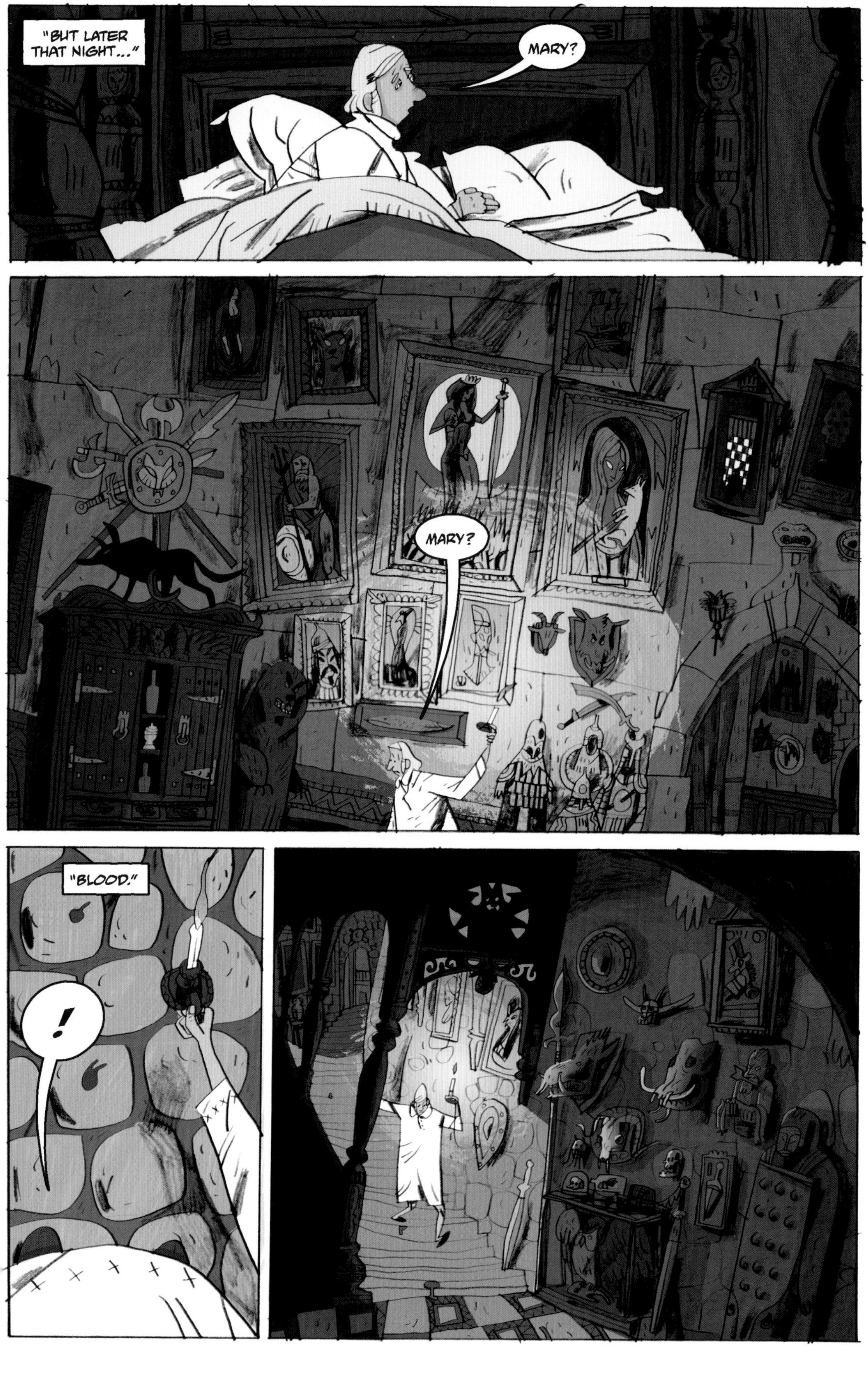
"BUT LATER THAT NIGHT..."
MARY?
MARY?
"BLOOD."
!

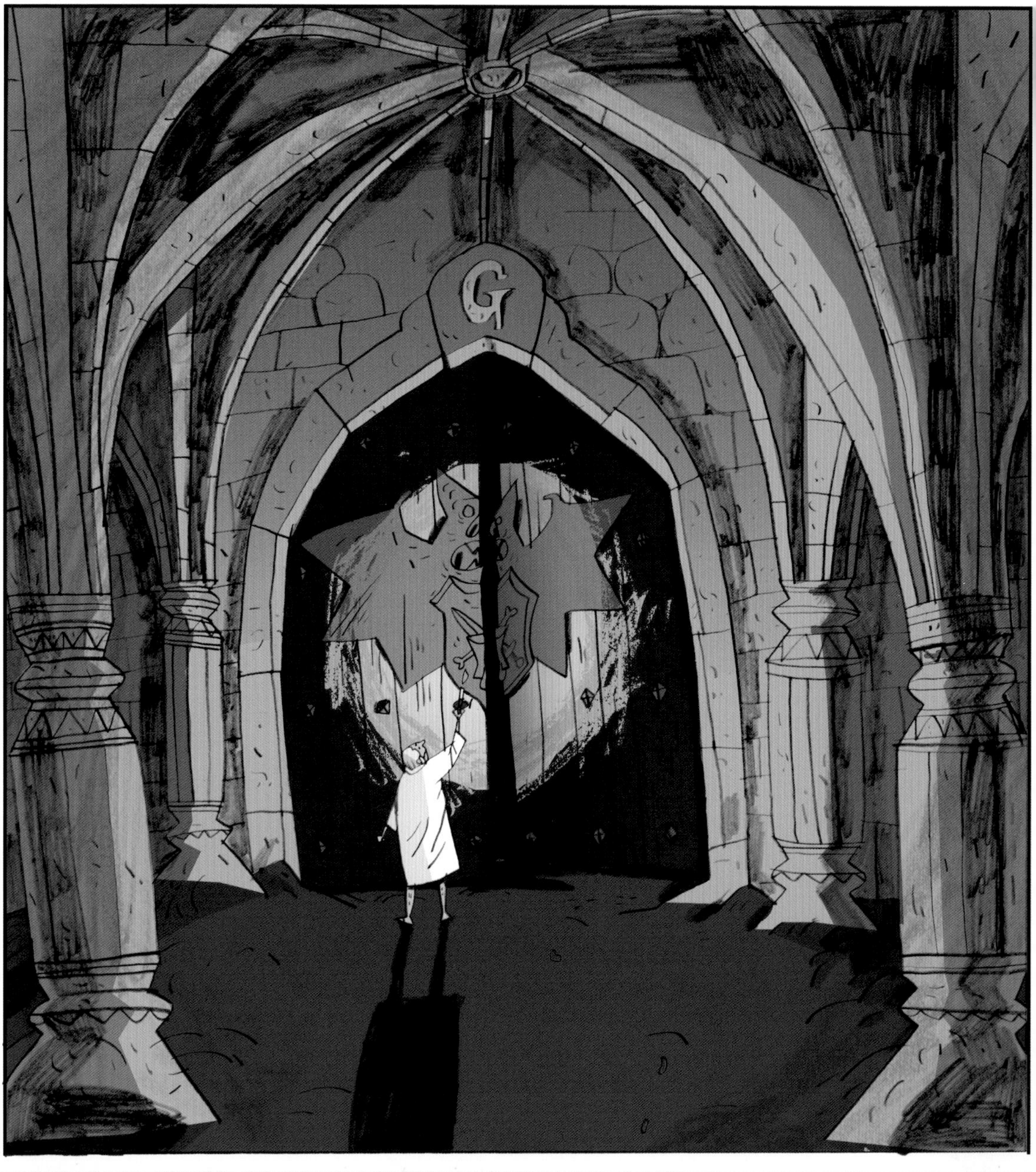

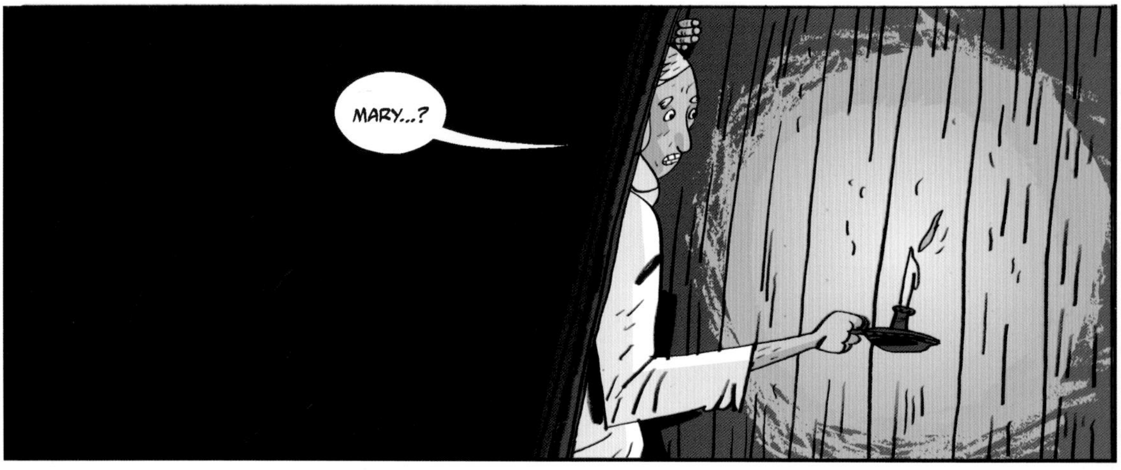
MARY...?

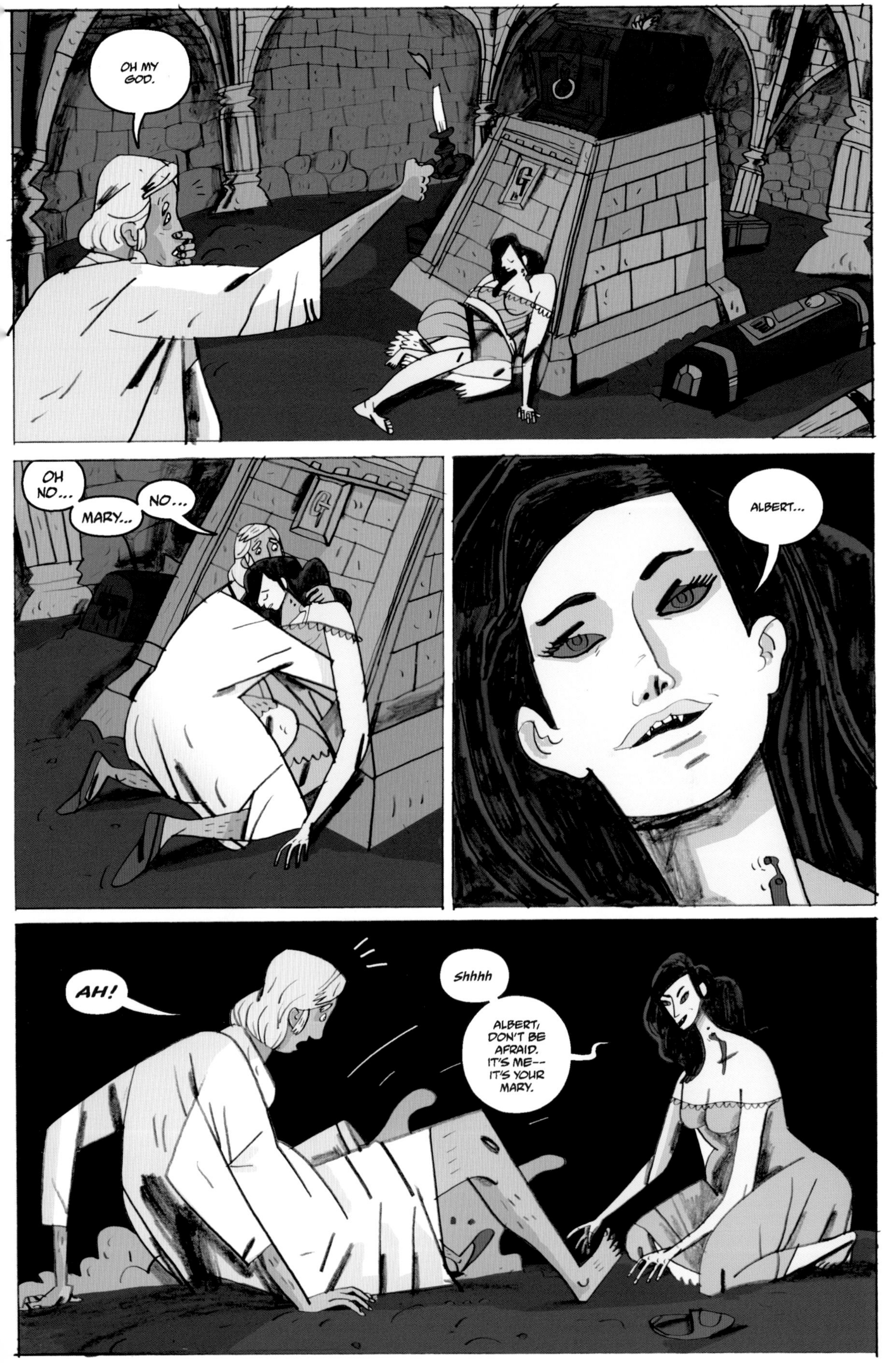
OH MY GOD.
OH NO...
MARY...
NO...
ALBERT...
AH!
Shhhh
ALBERT, DON'T BE AFRAID. IT'S ME-- IT'S YOUR MARY.

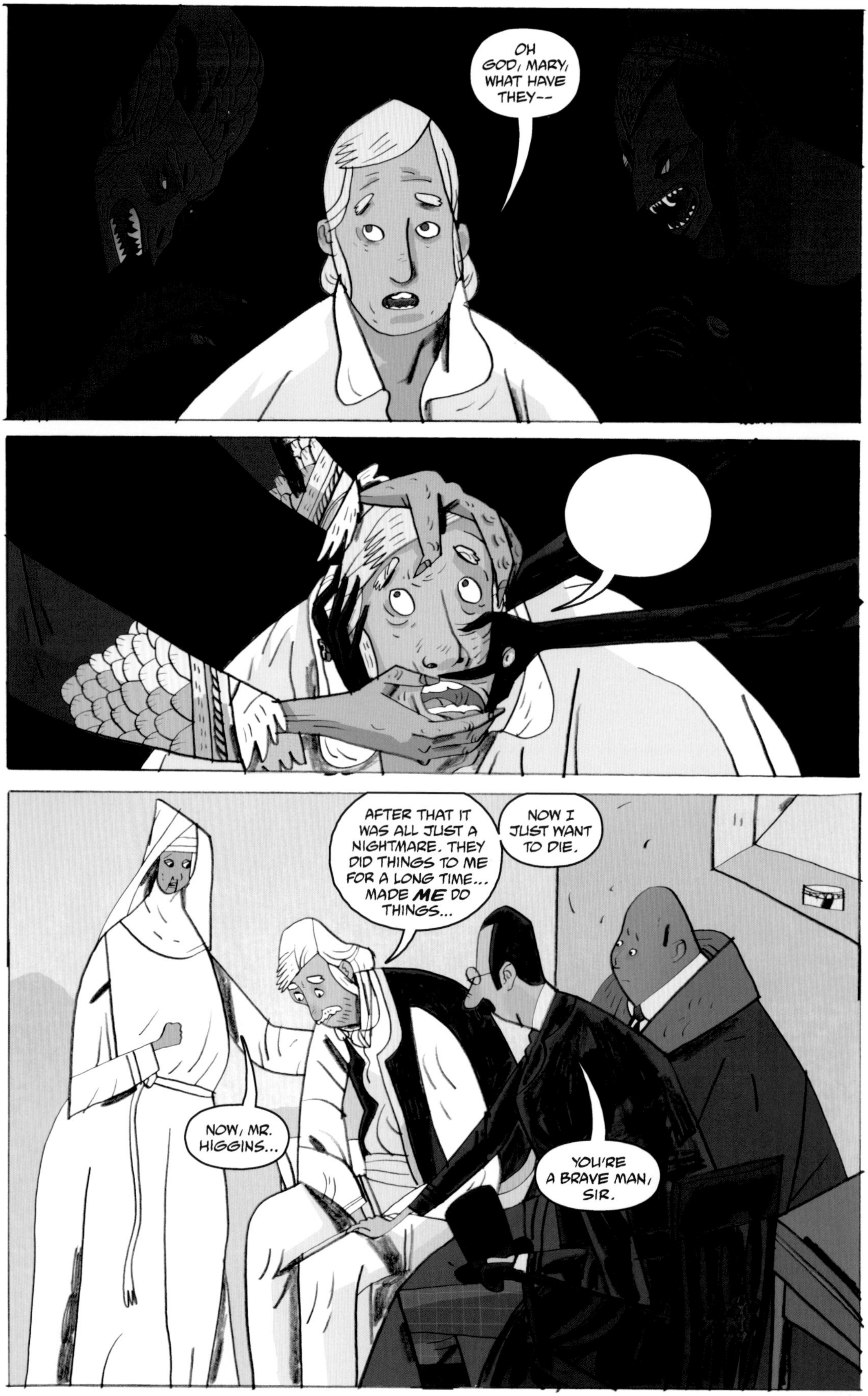
OH GOD, MARY, WHAT HAVE THEY--
AFTER THAT IT WAS ALL JUST A NIGHTMARE. THEY DID THINGS TO ME FOR A LONG TIME... MADE **ME** DO THINGS...
NOW I JUST WANT TO DIE.
NOW, MR. HIGGINS...
YOU'RE A BRAVE MAN, SIR.

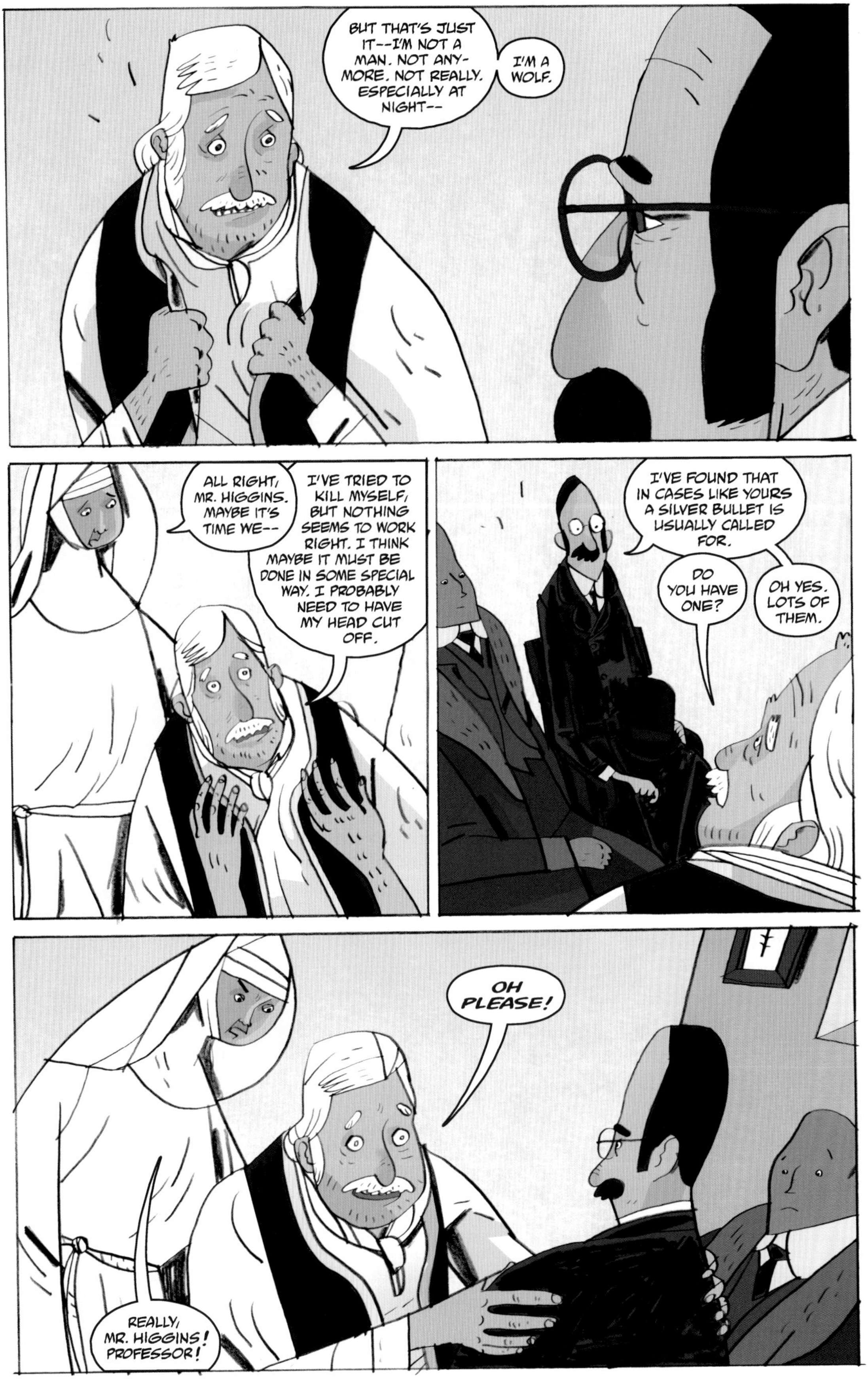
BUT THAT'S JUST IT--I'M NOT A MAN. NOT ANY-MORE. NOT REALLY. ESPECIALLY AT NIGHT--
I'M A WOLF.
ALL RIGHT, MR. HIGGINS. MAYBE IT'S TIME WE--
I'VE TRIED TO KILL MYSELF, BUT NOTHING SEEMS TO WORK RIGHT. I THINK MAYBE IT MUST BE DONE IN SOME SPECIAL WAY. I PROBABLY NEED TO HAVE MY HEAD CUT OFF.
I'VE FOUND THAT IN CASES LIKE YOURS A SILVER BULLET IS USUALLY CALLED FOR.
DO YOU HAVE ONE?
OH YES. LOTS OF THEM.
OH PLEASE!
REALLY, MR. HIGGINS! PROFESSOR!

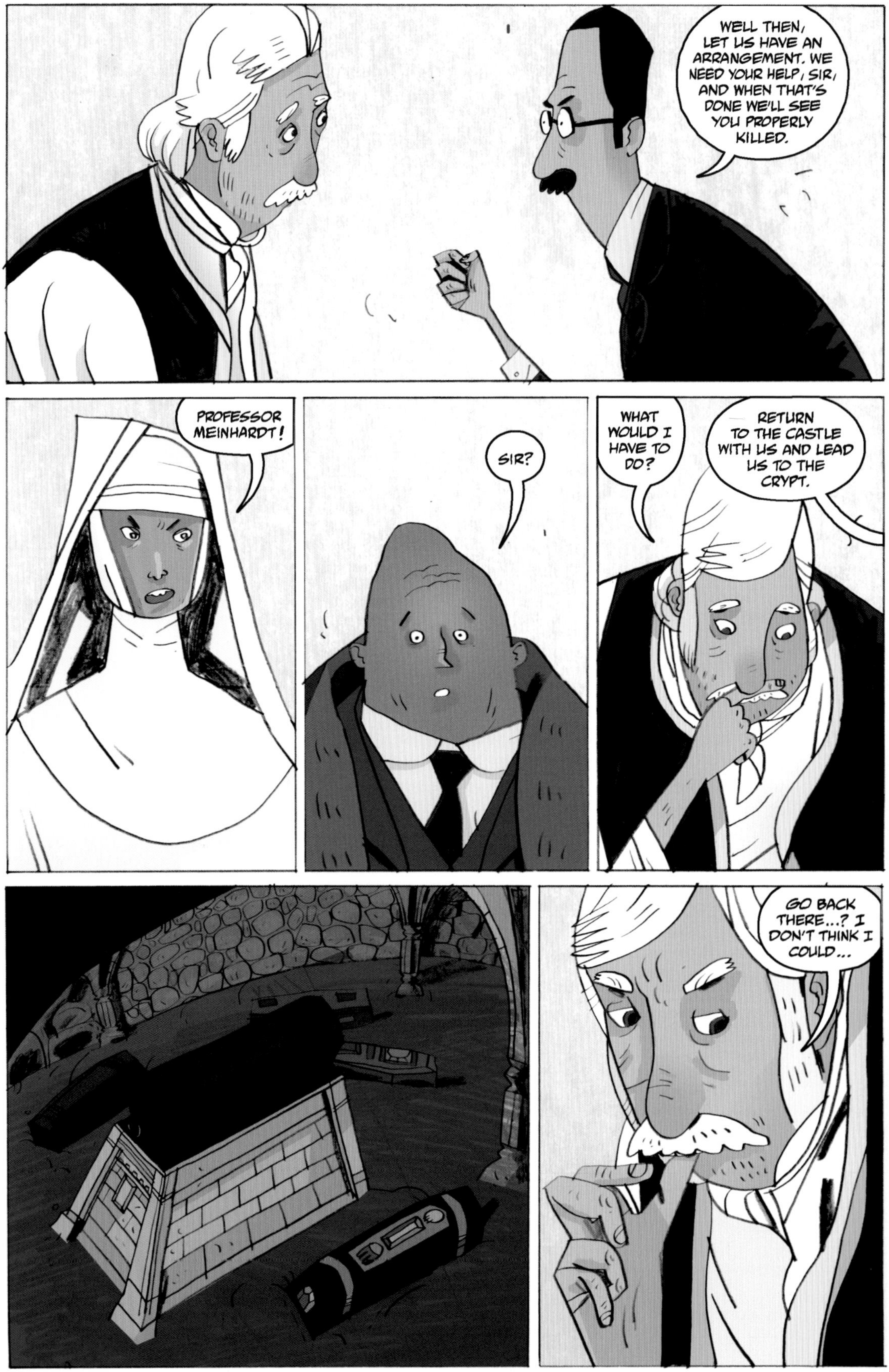
WELL THEN, LET US HAVE AN ARRANGEMENT. WE NEED YOUR HELP, SIR, AND WHEN THAT'S DONE WE'LL SEE YOU PROPERLY KILLED.
PROFESSOR MEINHARDT!
SIR?
WHAT WOULD I HAVE TO DO?
RETURN TO THE CASTLE WITH US AND LEAD US TO THE CRYPT.
GO BACK THERE...? I DON'T THINK I COULD...

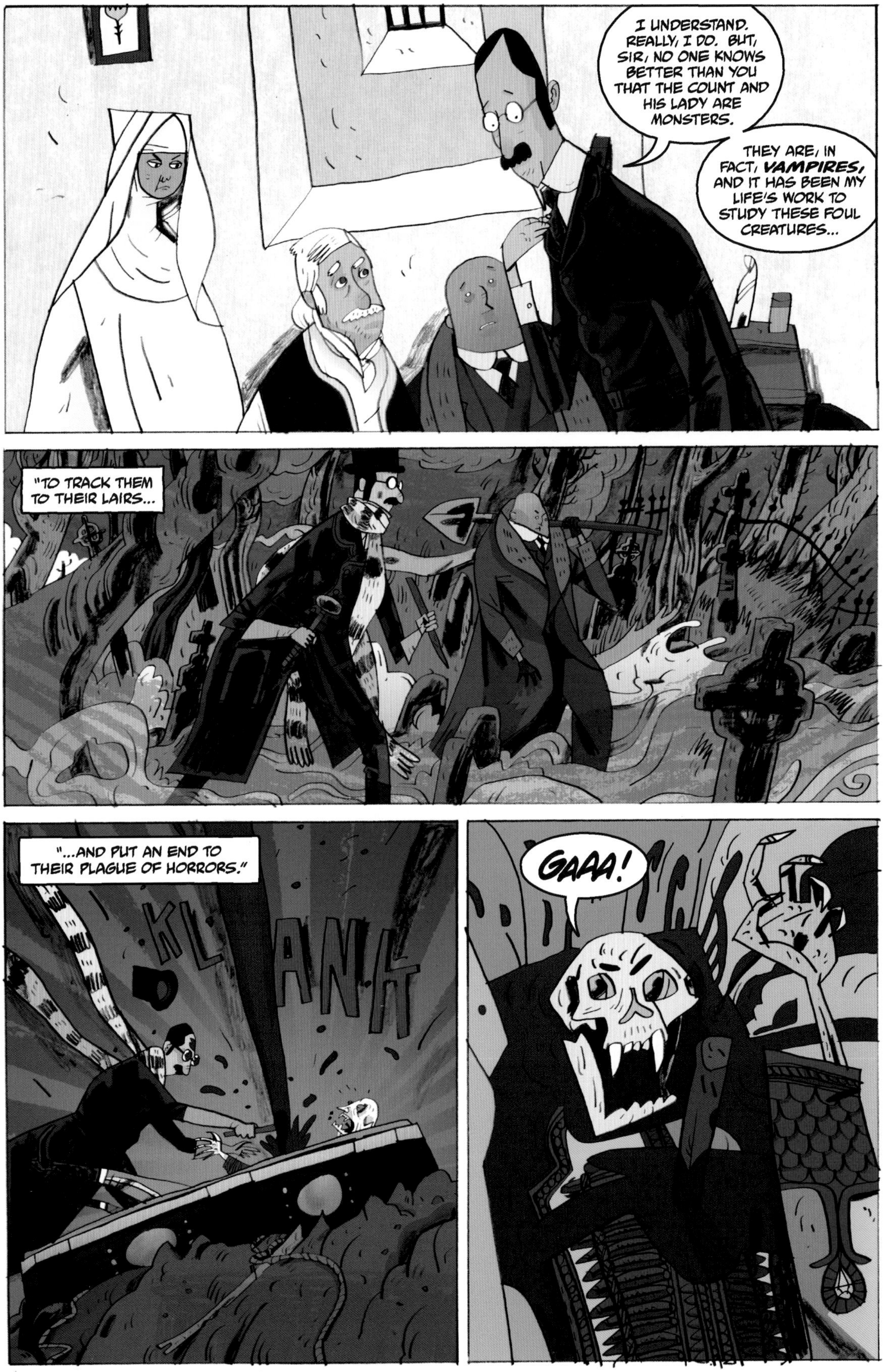
I UNDERSTAND. REALLY, I DO. BUT, SIR, NO ONE KNOWS BETTER THAN YOU THAT THE COUNT AND HIS LADY ARE MONSTERS.
THEY ARE, IN FACT, **VAMPIRES,** AND IT HAS BEEN MY LIFE'S WORK TO STUDY THESE FOUL CREATURES...
"TO TRACK THEM TO THEIR LAIRS...
"...AND PUT AN END TO THEIR PLAGUE OF HORRORS."
KLANK
GAAA!

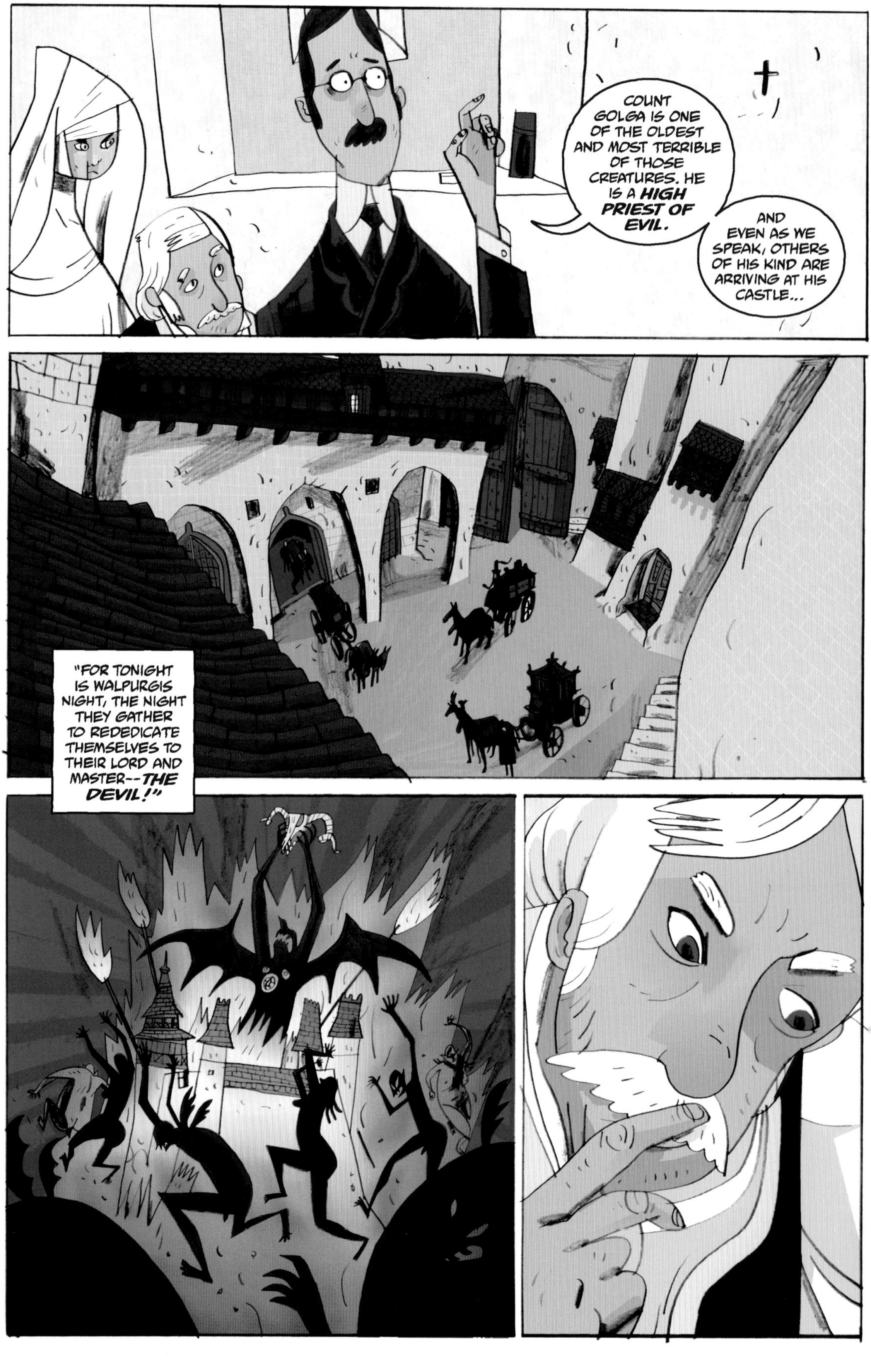
COUNT GOLGA IS ONE OF THE OLDEST AND MOST TERRIBLE OF THOSE CREATURES. HE IS A **HIGH PRIEST OF EVIL.**
AND EVEN AS WE SPEAK, OTHERS OF HIS KIND ARE ARRIVING AT HIS CASTLE...
"FOR TONIGHT IS WALPURGIS NIGHT, THE NIGHT THEY GATHER TO REDEDICATE THEMSELVES TO THEIR LORD AND MASTER--**THE DEVIL!**"

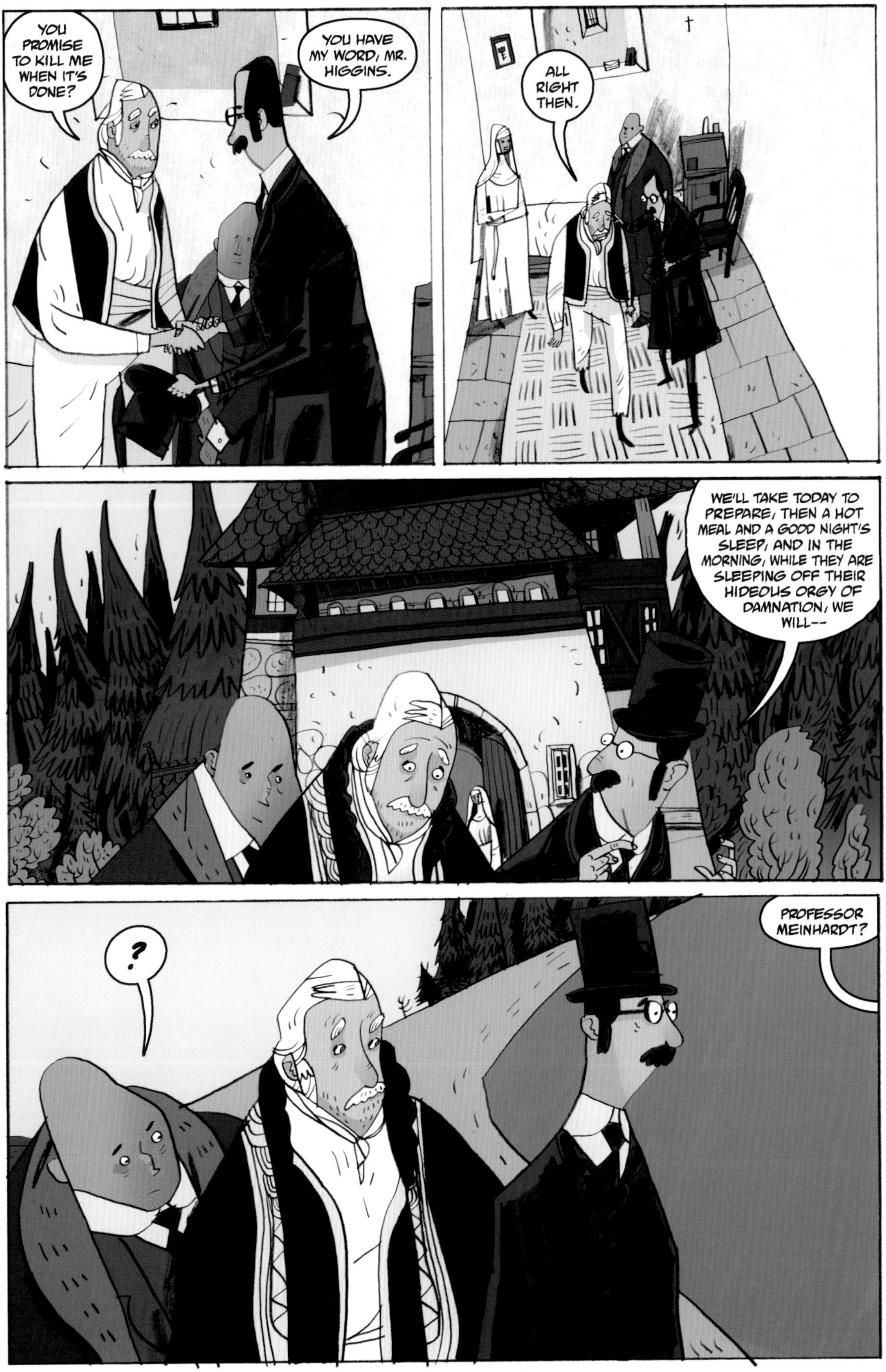
YOU PROMISE TO KILL ME WHEN IT'S DONE?
YOU HAVE MY WORD, MR. HIGGINS.
ALL RIGHT THEN.
WE'LL TAKE TODAY TO PREPARE, THEN A HOT MEAL AND A GOOD NIGHT'S SLEEP, AND IN THE MORNING, WHILE THEY ARE SLEEPING OFF THEIR HIDEOUS ORGY OF DAMNATION, WE WILL--
?
PROFESSOR MEINHARDT?

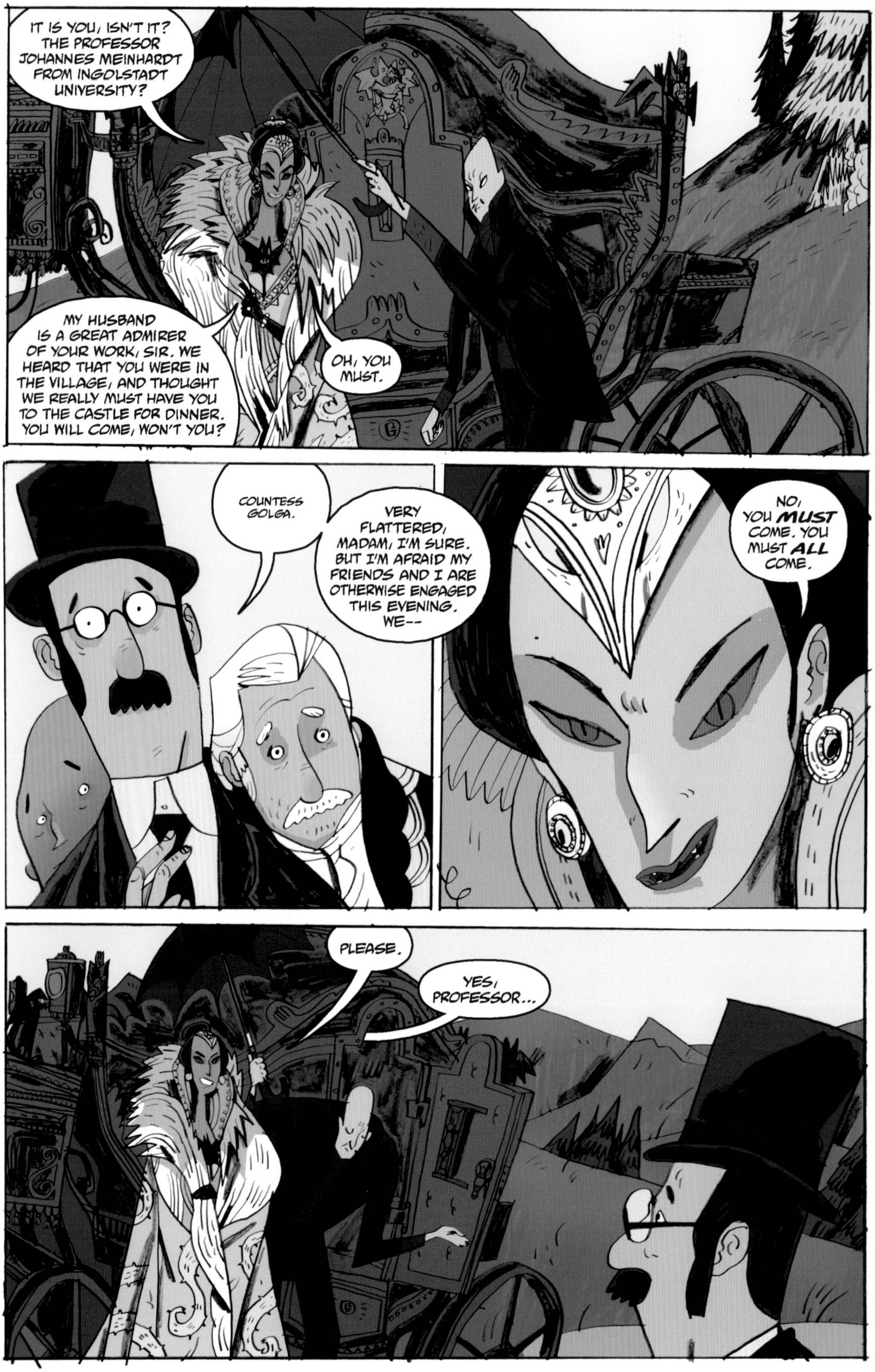
IT IS YOU, ISN'T IT? THE PROFESSOR JOHANNES MEINHARDT FROM INGOLSTADT UNIVERSITY?
MY HUSBAND IS A GREAT ADMIRER OF YOUR WORK, SIR. WE HEARD THAT YOU WERE IN THE VILLAGE, AND THOUGHT WE REALLY MUST HAVE YOU TO THE CASTLE FOR DINNER. YOU WILL COME, WON'T YOU?
OH, YOU MUST.
COUNTESS GOLGA.
VERY FLATTERED, MADAM, I'M SURE. BUT I'M AFRAID MY FRIENDS AND I ARE OTHERWISE ENGAGED THIS EVENING. WE--
NO, YOU **MUST** COME. YOU MUST **ALL** COME.
PLEASE.
YES, PROFESSOR...

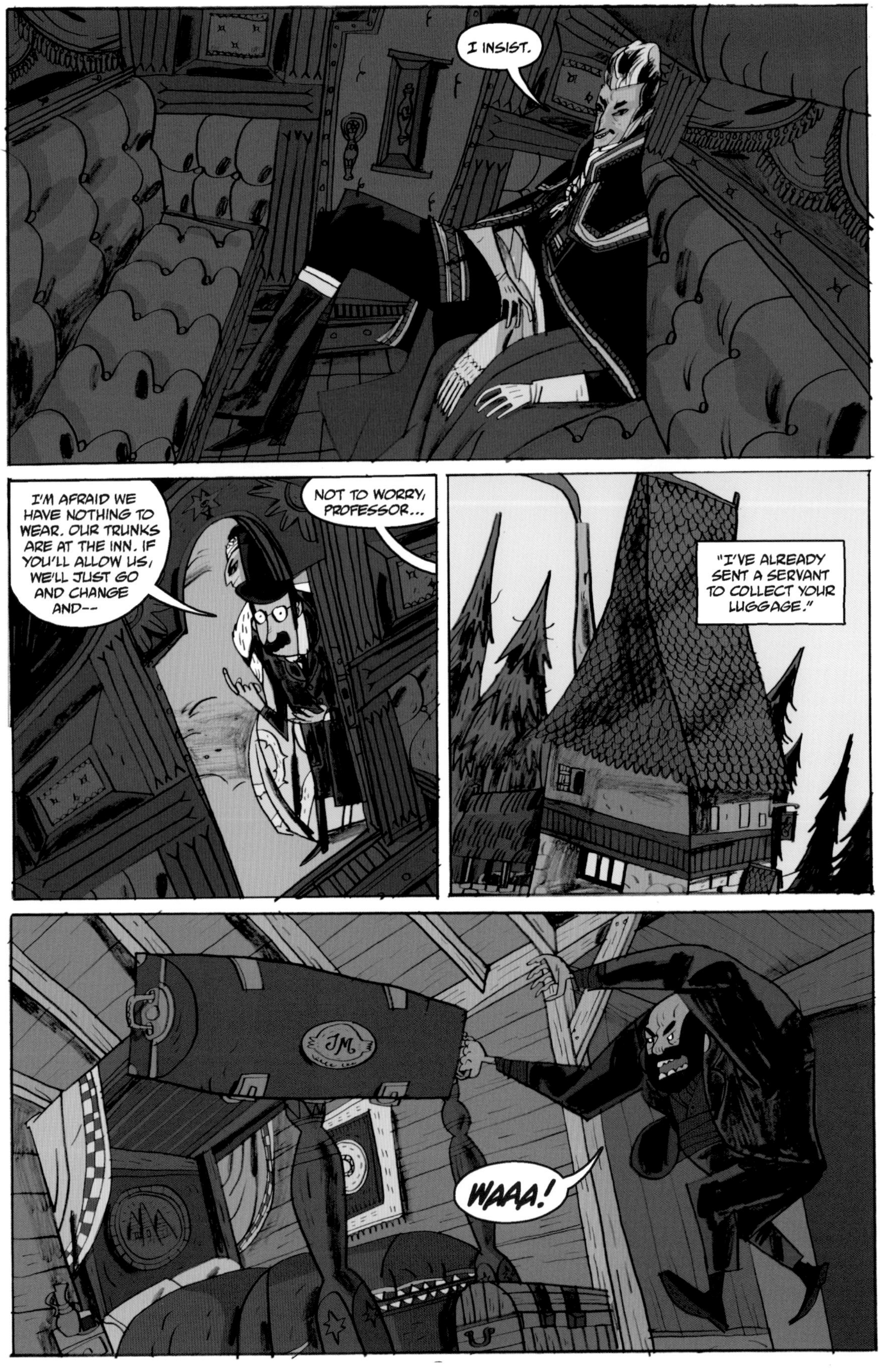
I INSIST.
I'M AFRAID WE HAVE NOTHING TO WEAR. OUR TRUNKS ARE AT THE INN. IF YOU'LL ALLOW US, WE'LL JUST GO AND CHANGE AND--
NOT TO WORRY, PROFESSOR...
"I'VE ALREADY SENT A SERVANT TO COLLECT YOUR LUGGAGE."
JM
WAAA!

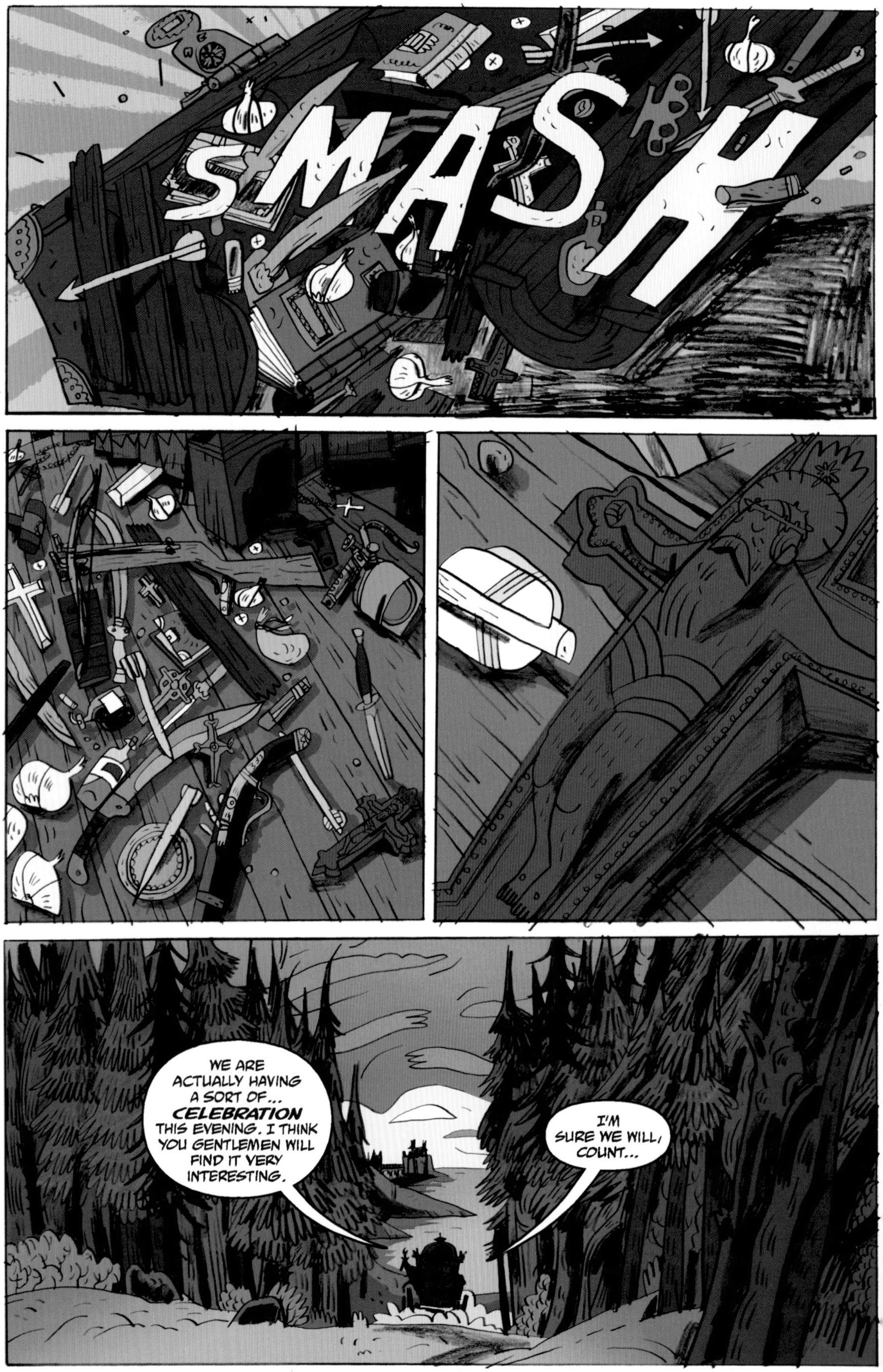
SMASH
WE ARE ACTUALLY HAVING A SORT OF... ***CELEBRATION*** THIS EVENING. I THINK YOU GENTLEMEN WILL FIND IT VERY INTERESTING.
I'M SURE WE WILL, COUNT...

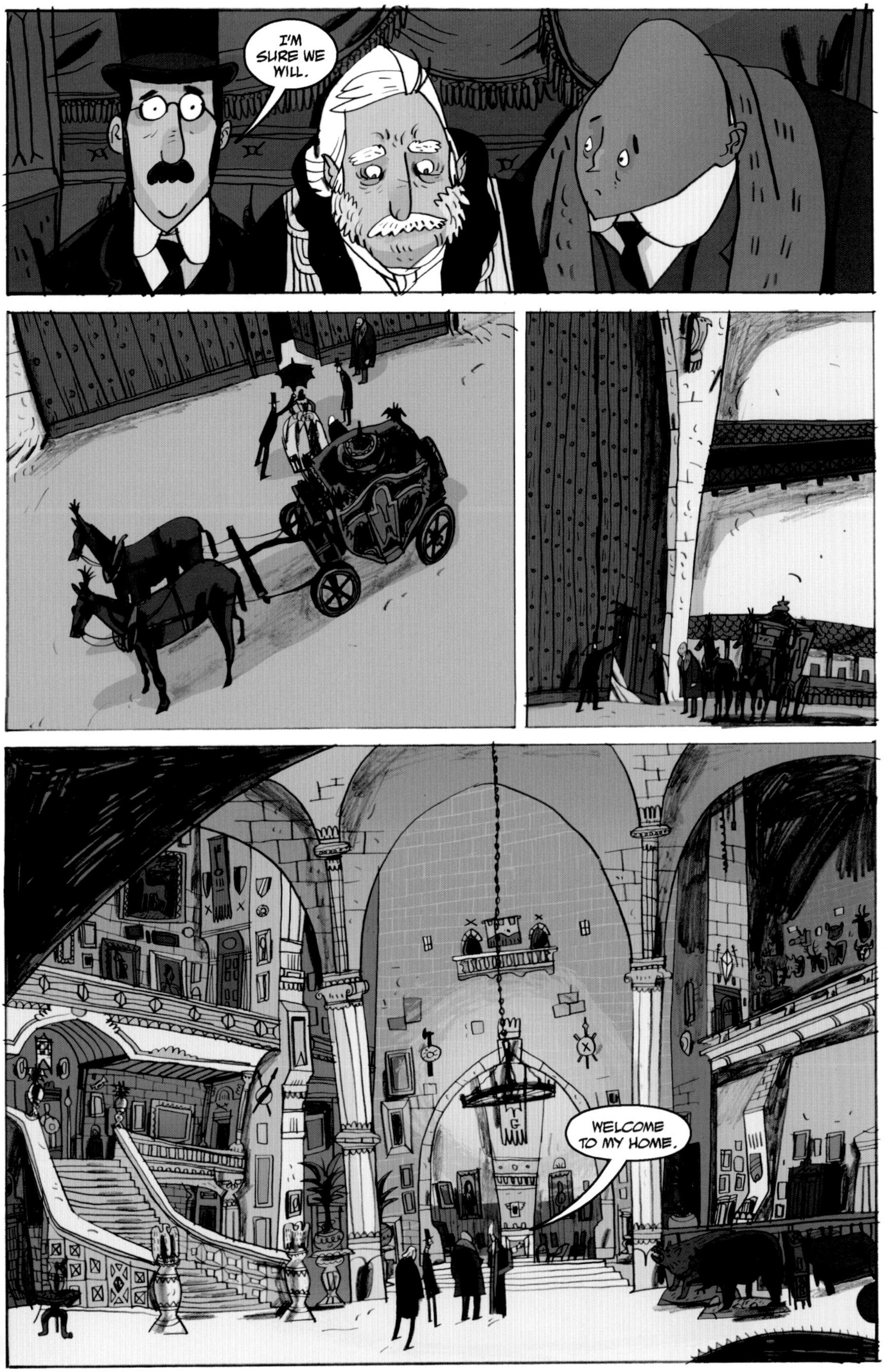
I'M SURE WE WILL.
WELCOME TO MY HOME.

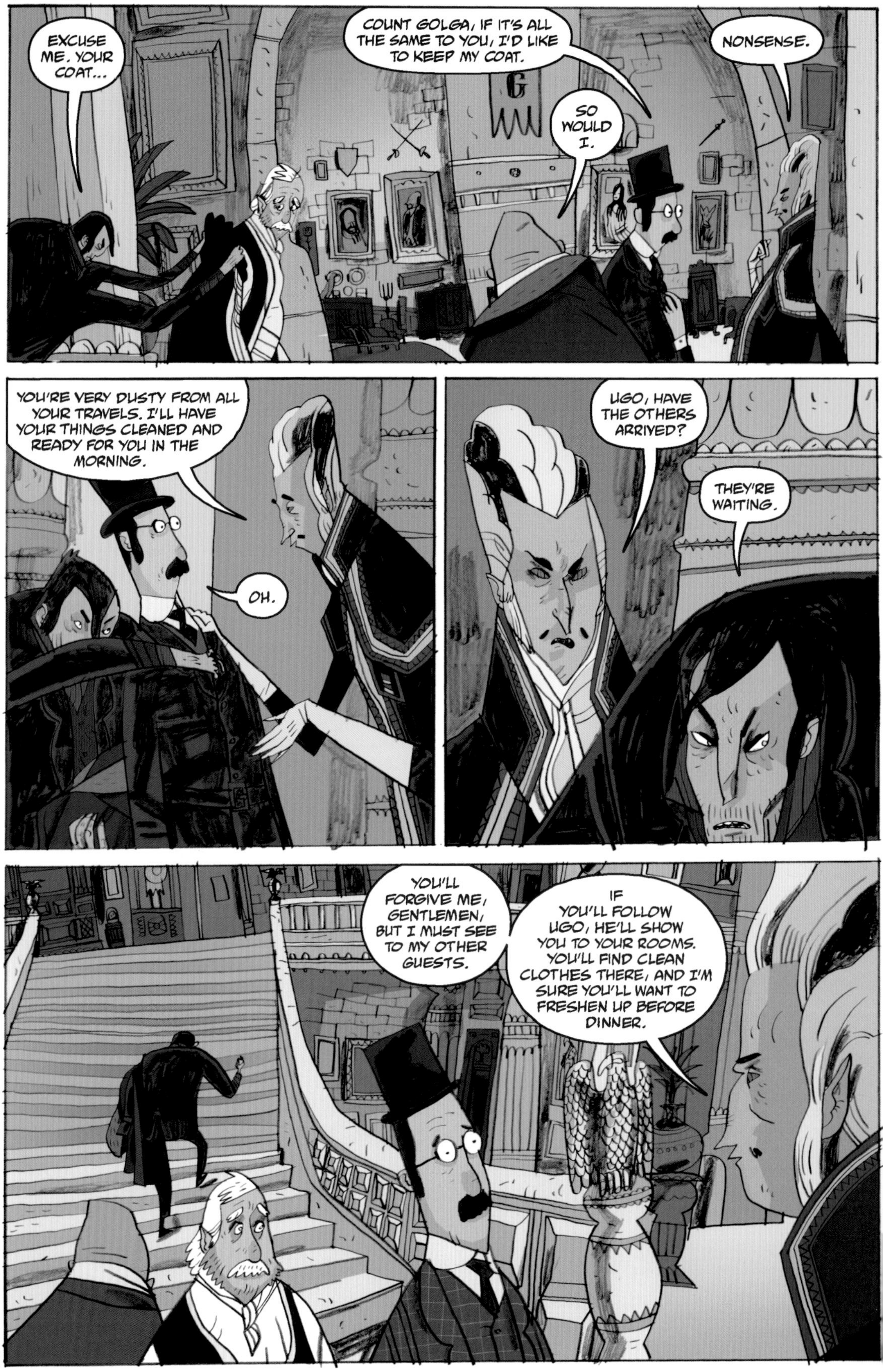
EXCUSE ME. YOUR COAT...
COUNT GOLGA, IF IT'S ALL THE SAME TO YOU, I'D LIKE TO KEEP MY COAT.
SO WOULD I.
NONSENSE.
YOU'RE VERY DUSTY FROM ALL YOUR TRAVELS. I'LL HAVE YOUR THINGS CLEANED AND READY FOR YOU IN THE MORNING.
OH.
UGO, HAVE THE OTHERS ARRIVED?
THEY'RE WAITING.
YOU'LL FORGIVE ME, GENTLEMEN, BUT I MUST SEE TO MY OTHER GUESTS.
IF YOU'LL FOLLOW UGO, HE'LL SHOW YOU TO YOUR ROOMS. YOU'LL FIND CLEAN CLOTHES THERE, AND I'M SURE YOU'LL WANT TO FRESHEN UP BEFORE DINNER.

I'LL SEE YOU ALL SHORTLY.
THIS WAY.
PROFESSOR...?
NOT NOW.
WELCOME, FRIENDS, ONE AND ALL.
WELL MET, NOW AND FOREVER, EVEN TO THE ENDING OF THE WORLD.
HEAR, HEAR!

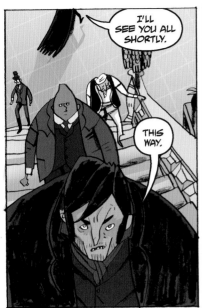

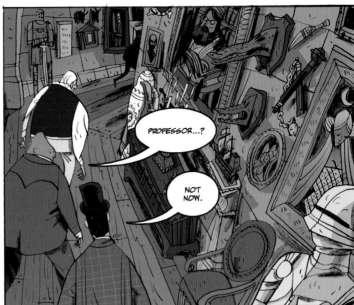

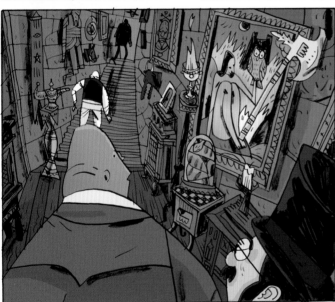

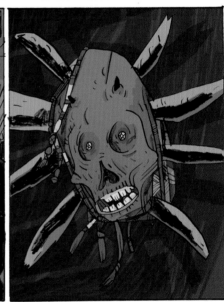

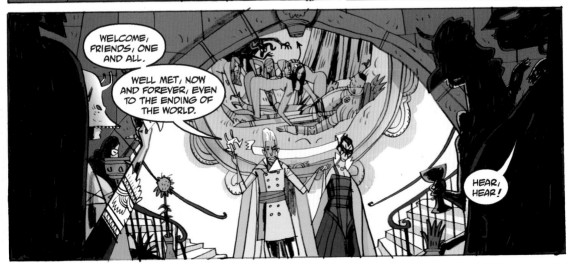

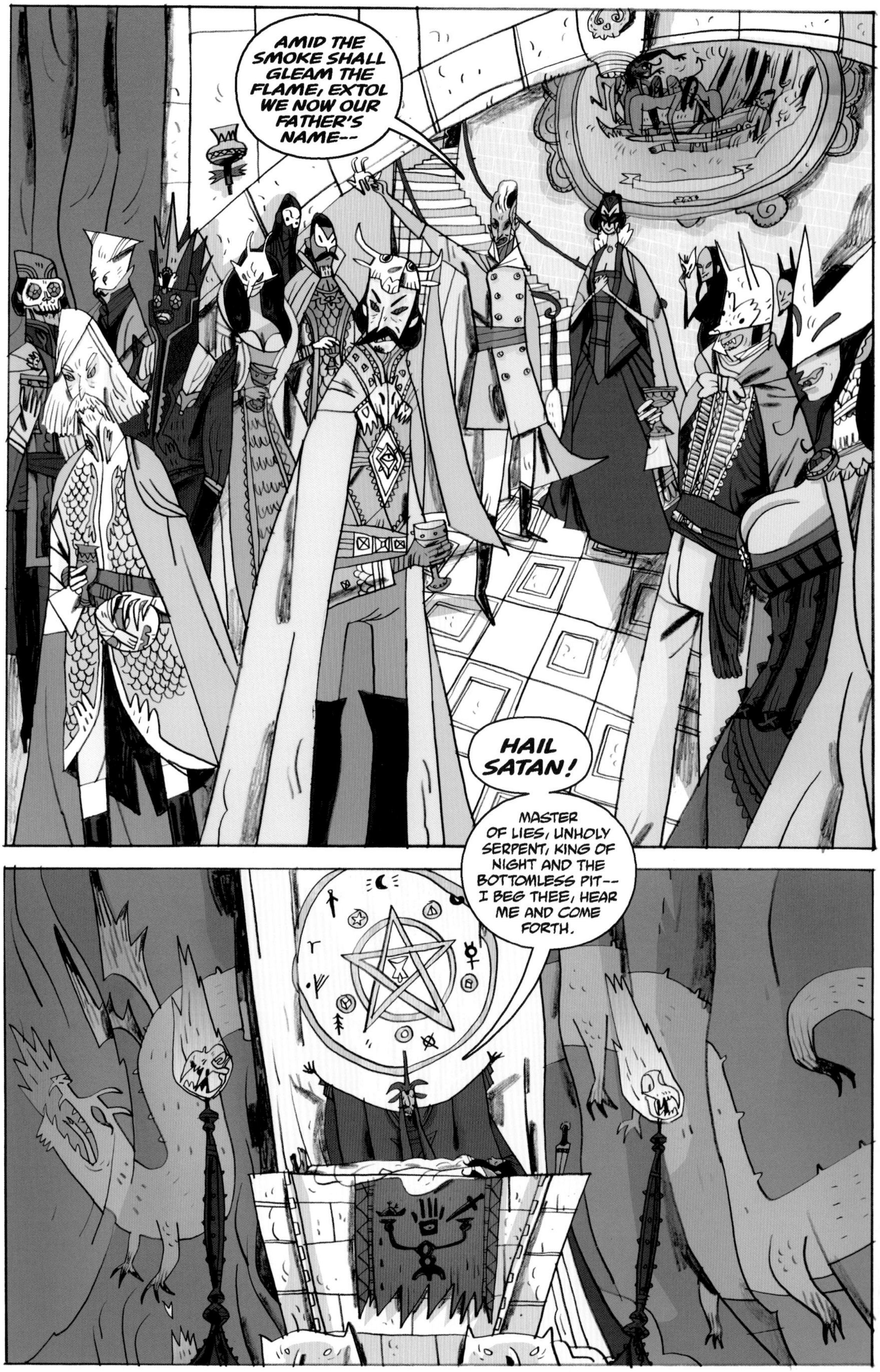
AMID THE SMOKE SHALL GLEAM THE FLAME, EXTOL WE NOW OUR FATHER'S NAME--
HAIL SATAN!
MASTER OF LIES, UNHOLY SERPENT, KING OF NIGHT AND THE BOTTOMLESS PIT-- I BEG THEE, HEAR ME AND COME FORTH.

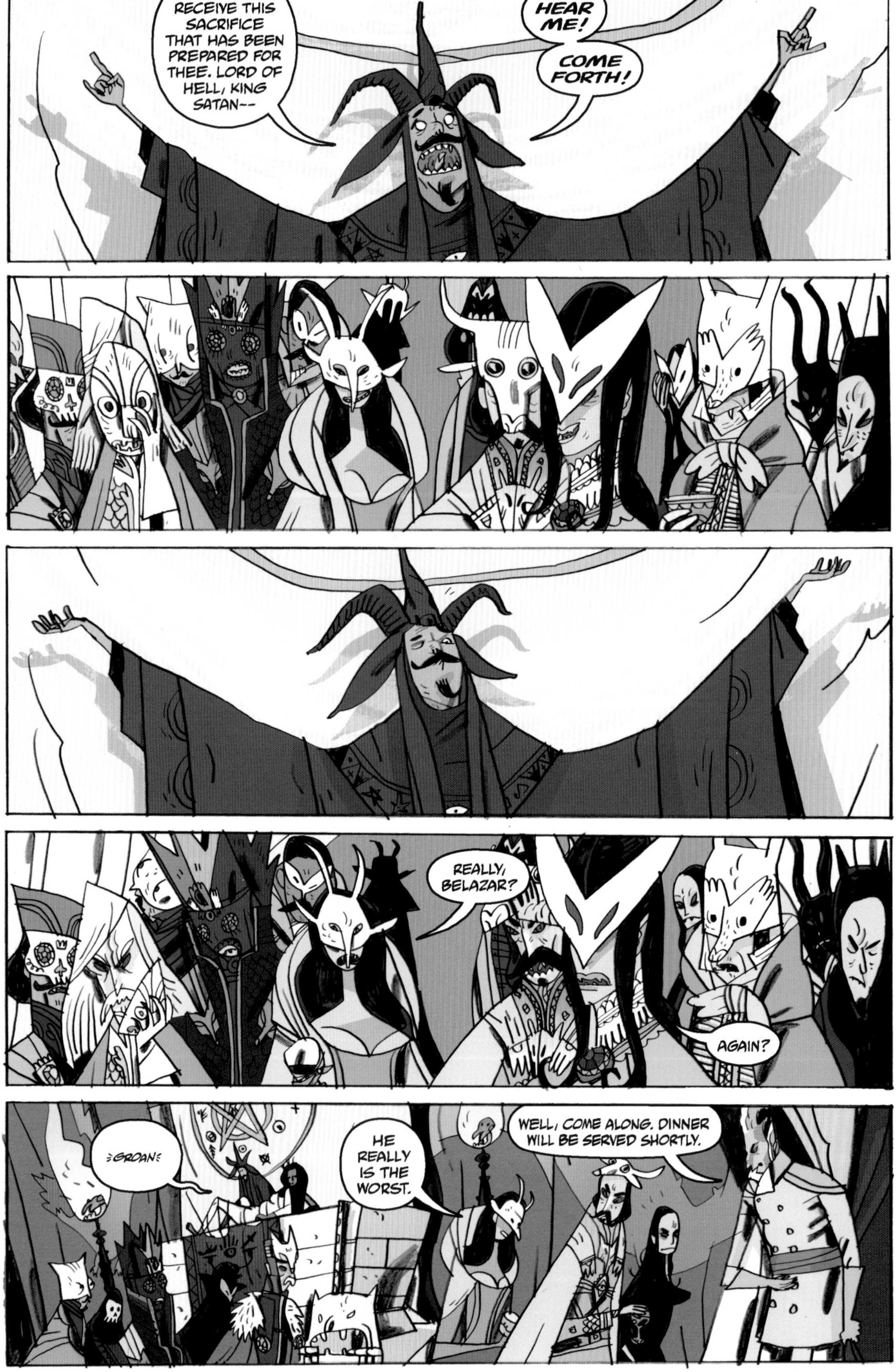
RECEIVE THIS SACRIFICE THAT HAS BEEN PREPARED FOR THEE. LORD OF HELL, KING SATAN--
HEAR ME!
COME FORTH!
REALLY, BELAZAR?
AGAIN?
GROAN
HE REALLY IS THE WORST.
WELL, COME ALONG. DINNER WILL BE SERVED SHORTLY.

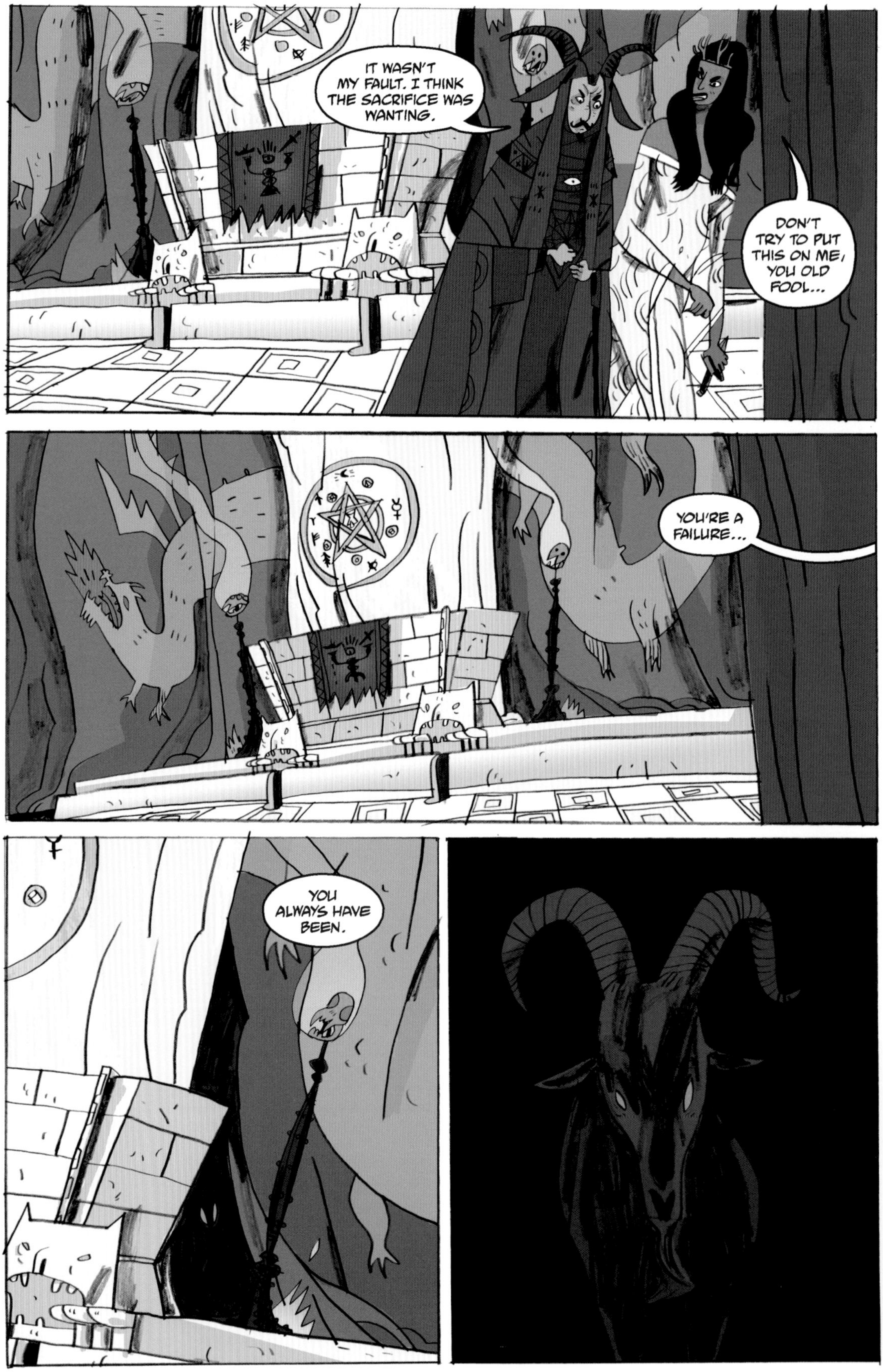
IT WASN'T MY FAULT. I THINK THE SACRIFICE WAS WANTING.
DON'T TRY TO PUT THIS ON ME, YOU OLD FOOL...
YOU'RE A FAILURE...
YOU ALWAYS HAVE BEEN.

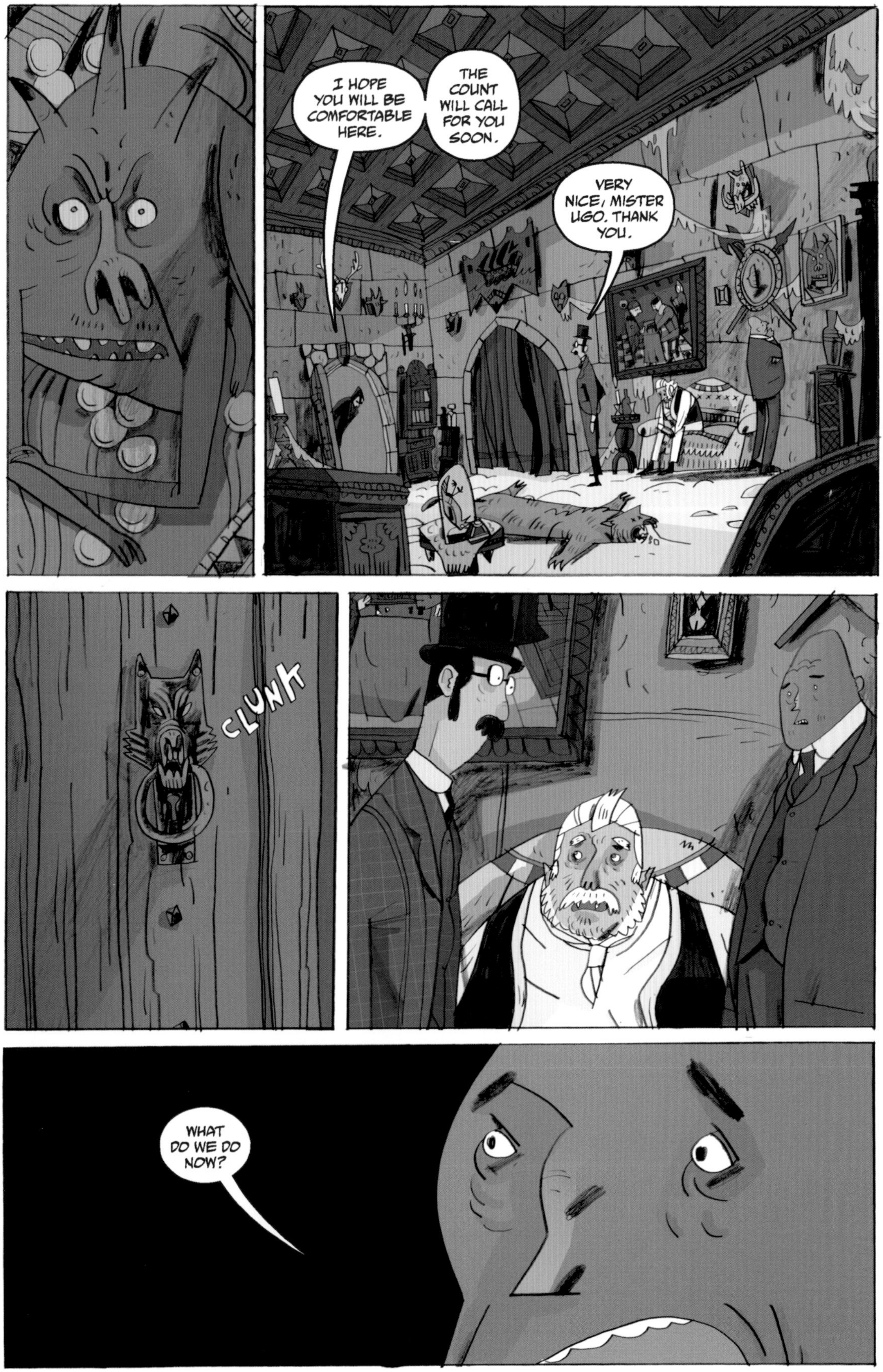
I HOPE YOU WILL BE COMFORTABLE HERE.
THE COUNT WILL CALL FOR YOU SOON.
VERY NICE, MISTER UGO. THANK YOU.
CLUNK
WHAT DO WE DO NOW?

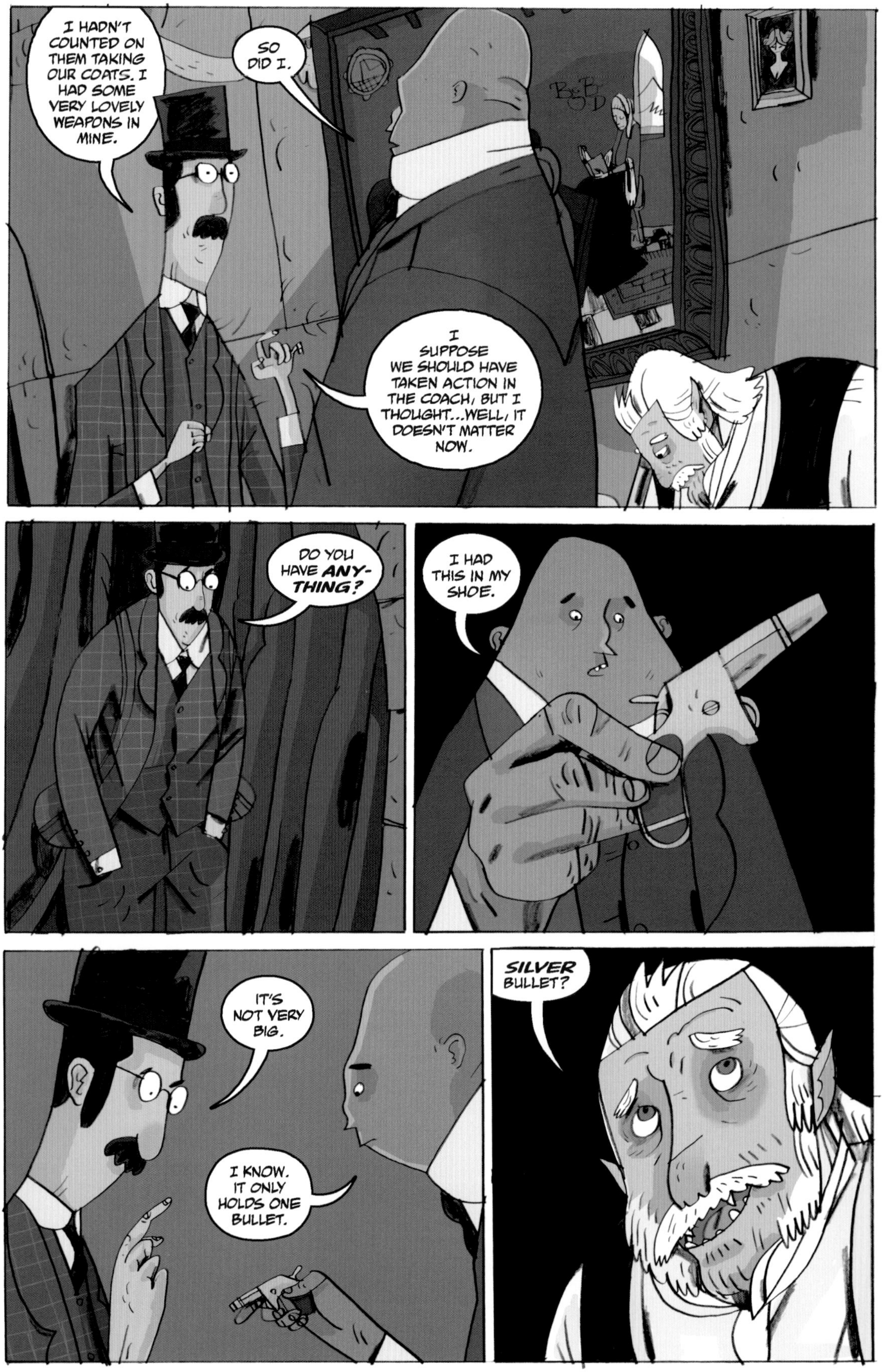
I HADN'T COUNTED ON THEM TAKING OUR COATS. I HAD SOME VERY LOVELY WEAPONS IN MINE.
SO DID I.
I SUPPOSE WE SHOULD HAVE TAKEN ACTION IN THE COACH, BUT I THOUGHT... WELL, IT DOESN'T MATTER NOW.
DO YOU HAVE **ANYTHING?**
I HAD THIS IN MY SHOE.
IT'S NOT VERY BIG.
I KNOW. IT ONLY HOLDS ONE BULLET.
SILVER BULLET?

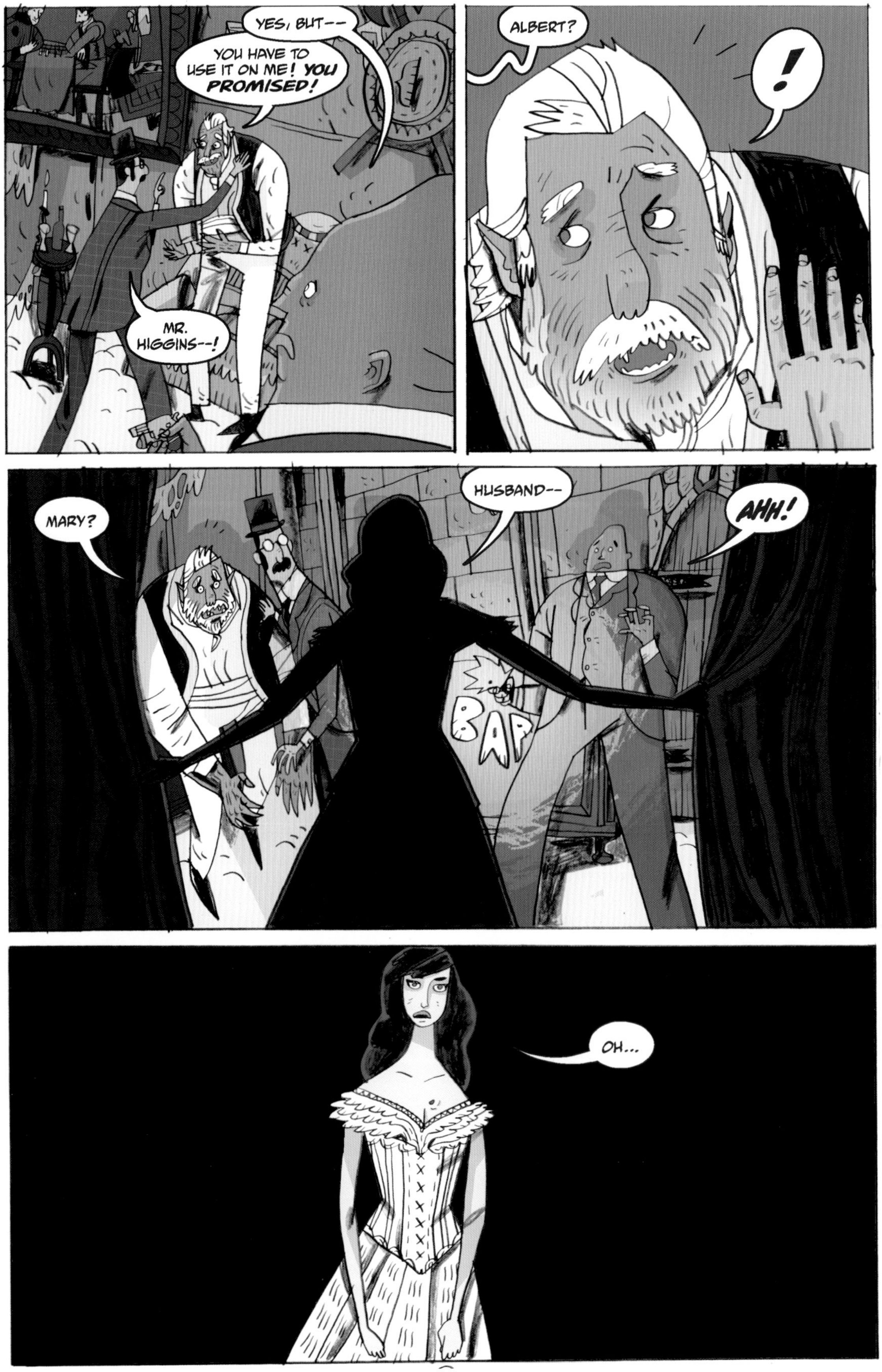
YES, BUT--
YOU HAVE TO USE IT ON ME! YOU PROMISED!
MR. HIGGINS--!
ALBERT?
!
MARY?
HUSBAND--
AHH!
BAP
OH...

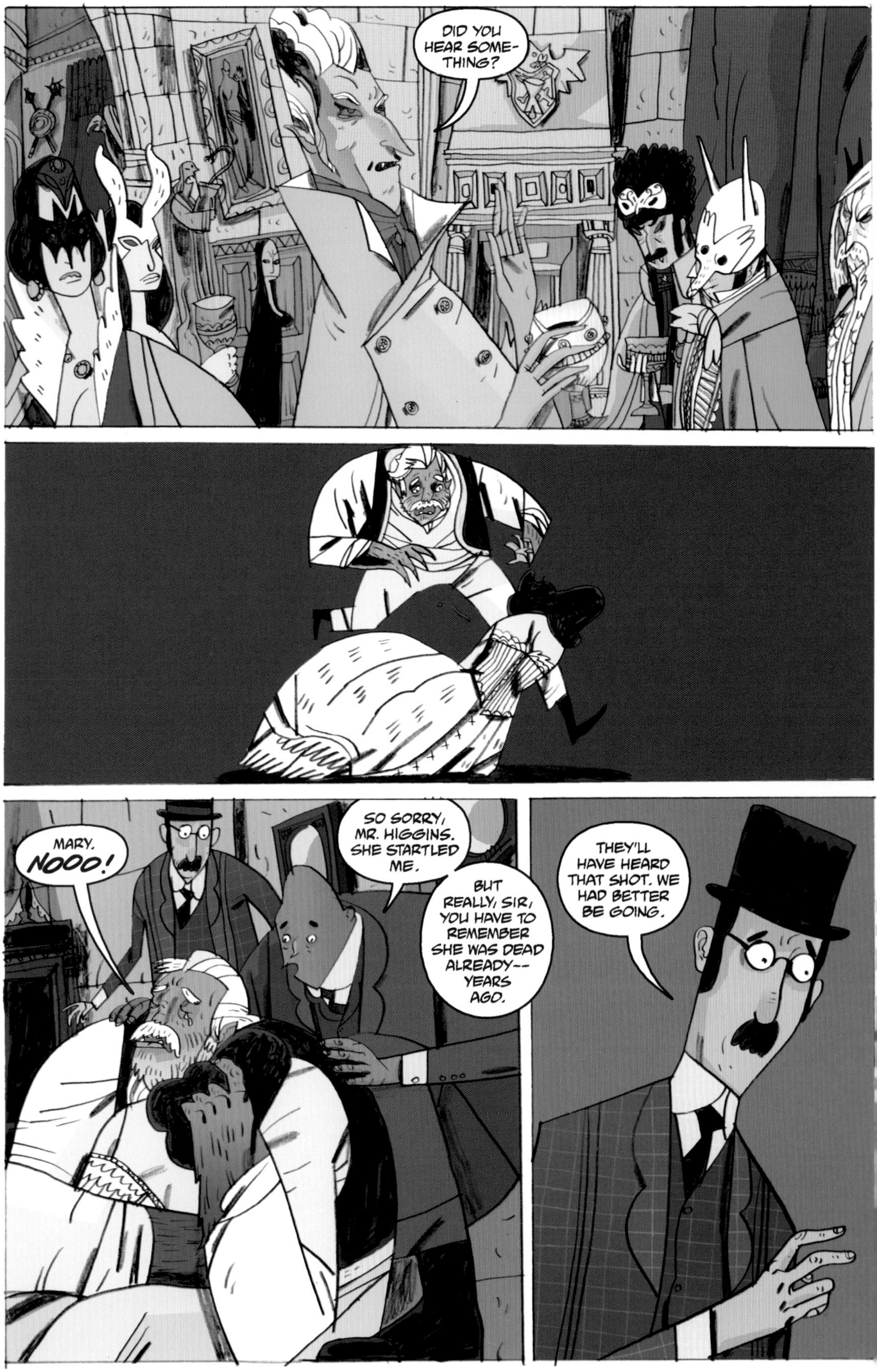

DID YOU HEAR SOME-THING?
MARY. NOOO!
SO SORRY, MR. HIGGINS. SHE STARTLED ME.
BUT REALLY, SIR, YOU HAVE TO REMEMBER SHE WAS DEAD ALREADY-- YEARS AGO.
THEY'LL HAVE HEARD THAT SHOT. WE HAD BETTER BE GOING.

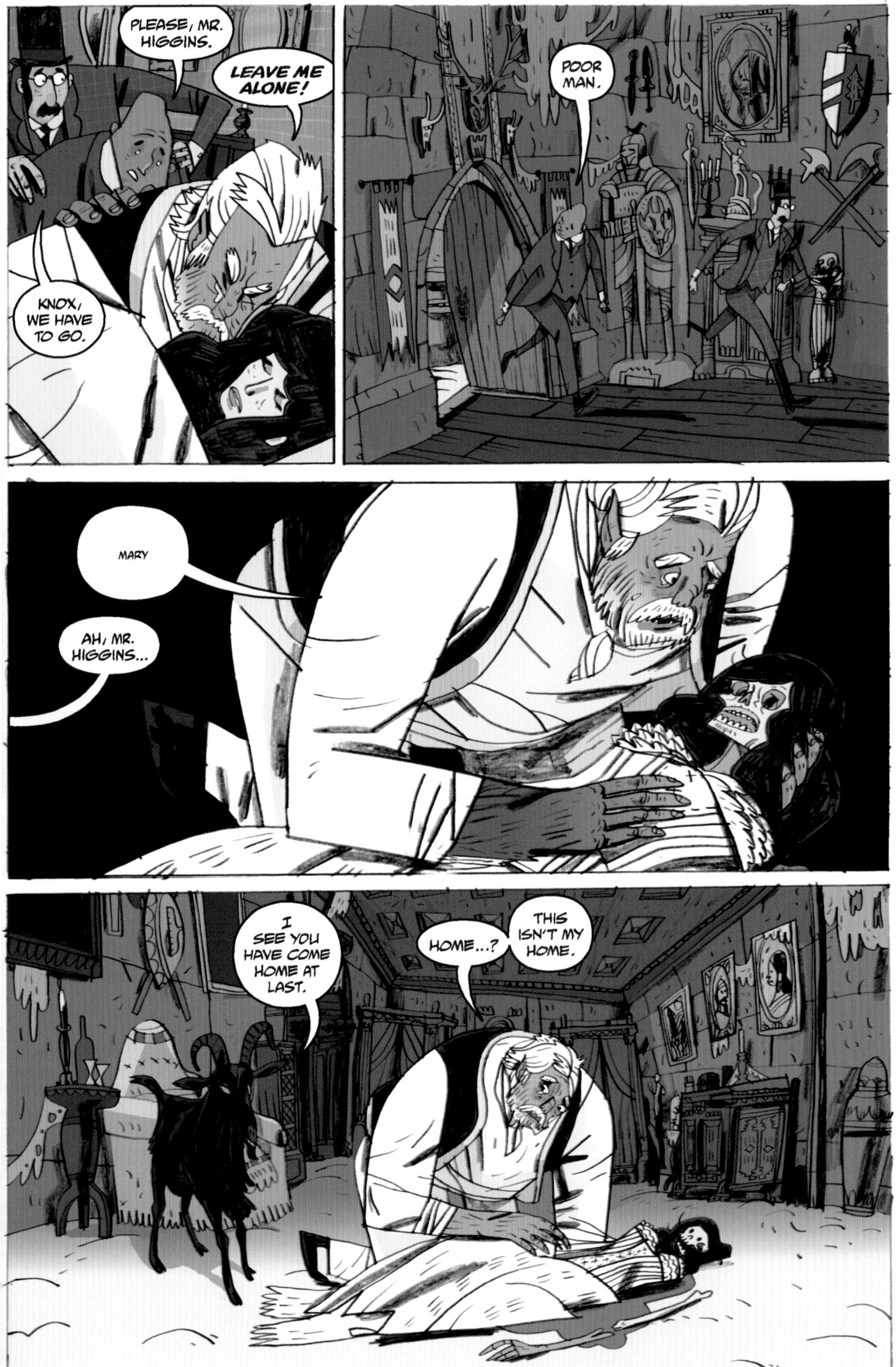
PLEASE, MR. HIGGINS.
LEAVE ME ALONE!
KNOX, WE HAVE TO GO.
POOR MAN.
MARY
AH, MR. HIGGINS...
I SEE YOU HAVE COME HOME AT LAST.
HOME...?
THIS ISN'T MY HOME.

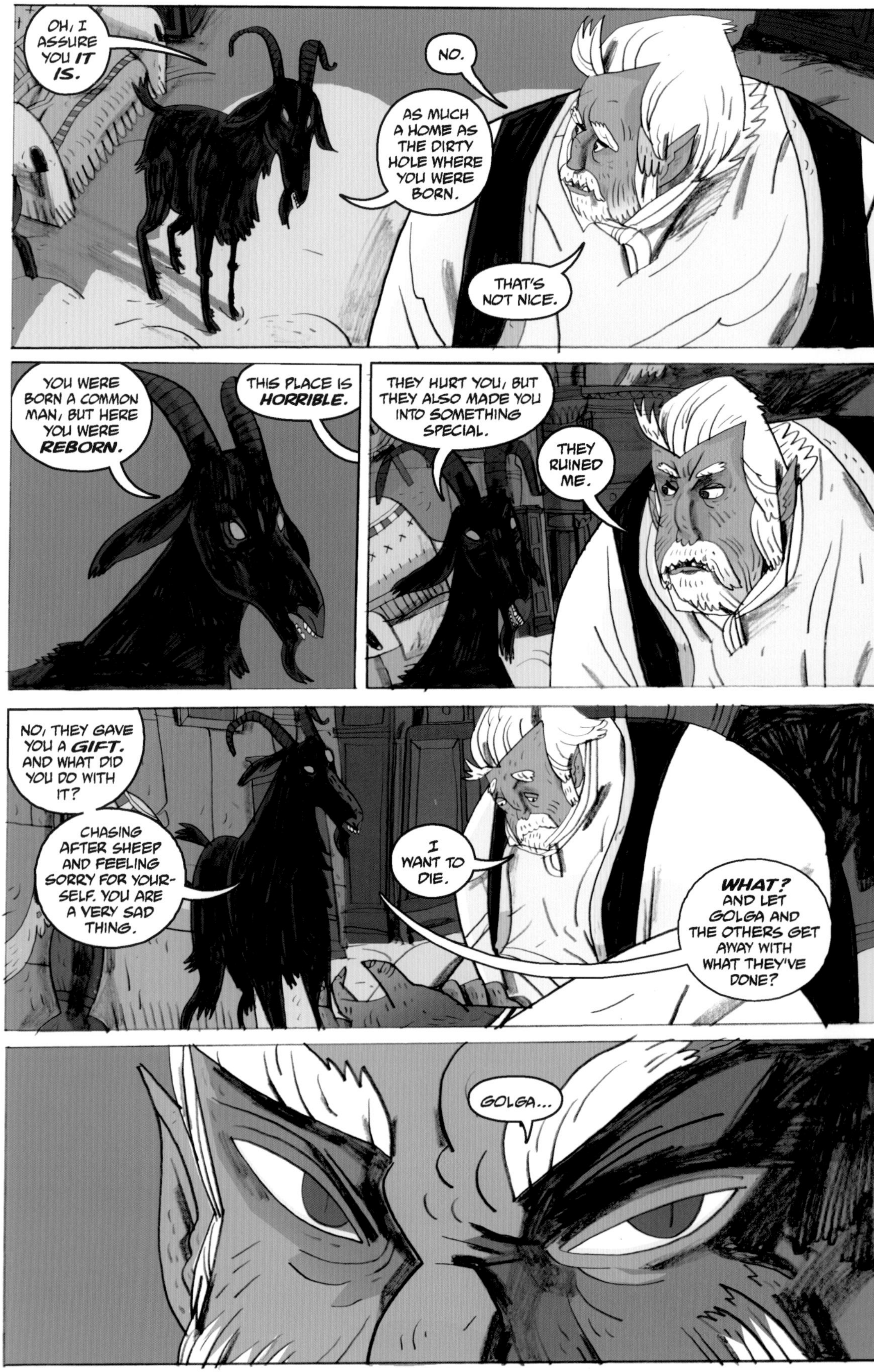
OH, I ASSURE YOU IT IS.
NO.
AS MUCH A HOME AS THE DIRTY HOLE WHERE YOU WERE BORN.
THAT'S NOT NICE.
YOU WERE BORN A COMMON MAN, BUT HERE YOU WERE REBORN.
THIS PLACE IS HORRIBLE.
THEY HURT YOU, BUT THEY ALSO MADE YOU INTO SOMETHING SPECIAL.
THEY RUINED ME.
NO, THEY GAVE YOU A GIFT. AND WHAT DID YOU DO WITH IT?
CHASING AFTER SHEEP AND FEELING SORRY FOR YOUR-SELF. YOU ARE A VERY SAD THING.
I WANT TO DIE.
WHAT? AND LET GOLGA AND THE OTHERS GET AWAY WITH WHAT THEY'VE DONE?
GOLGA...

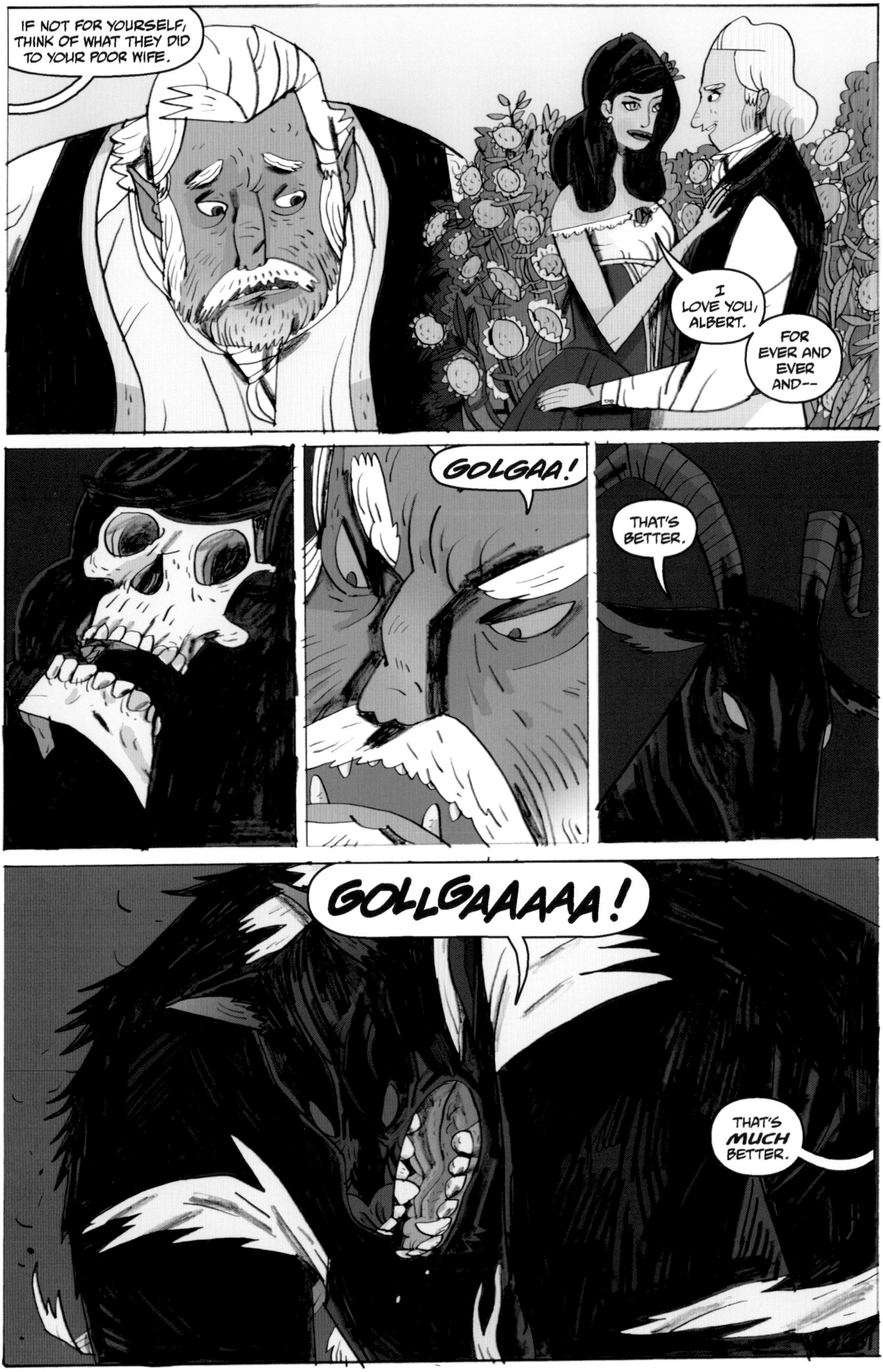
IF NOT FOR YOURSELF, THINK OF WHAT THEY DID TO YOUR POOR WIFE.
I LOVE YOU, ALBERT.
FOR EVER AND EVER AND--
GOLGAA!
THAT'S BETTER.
GOLLGAAAAA!
THAT'S MUCH BETTER.

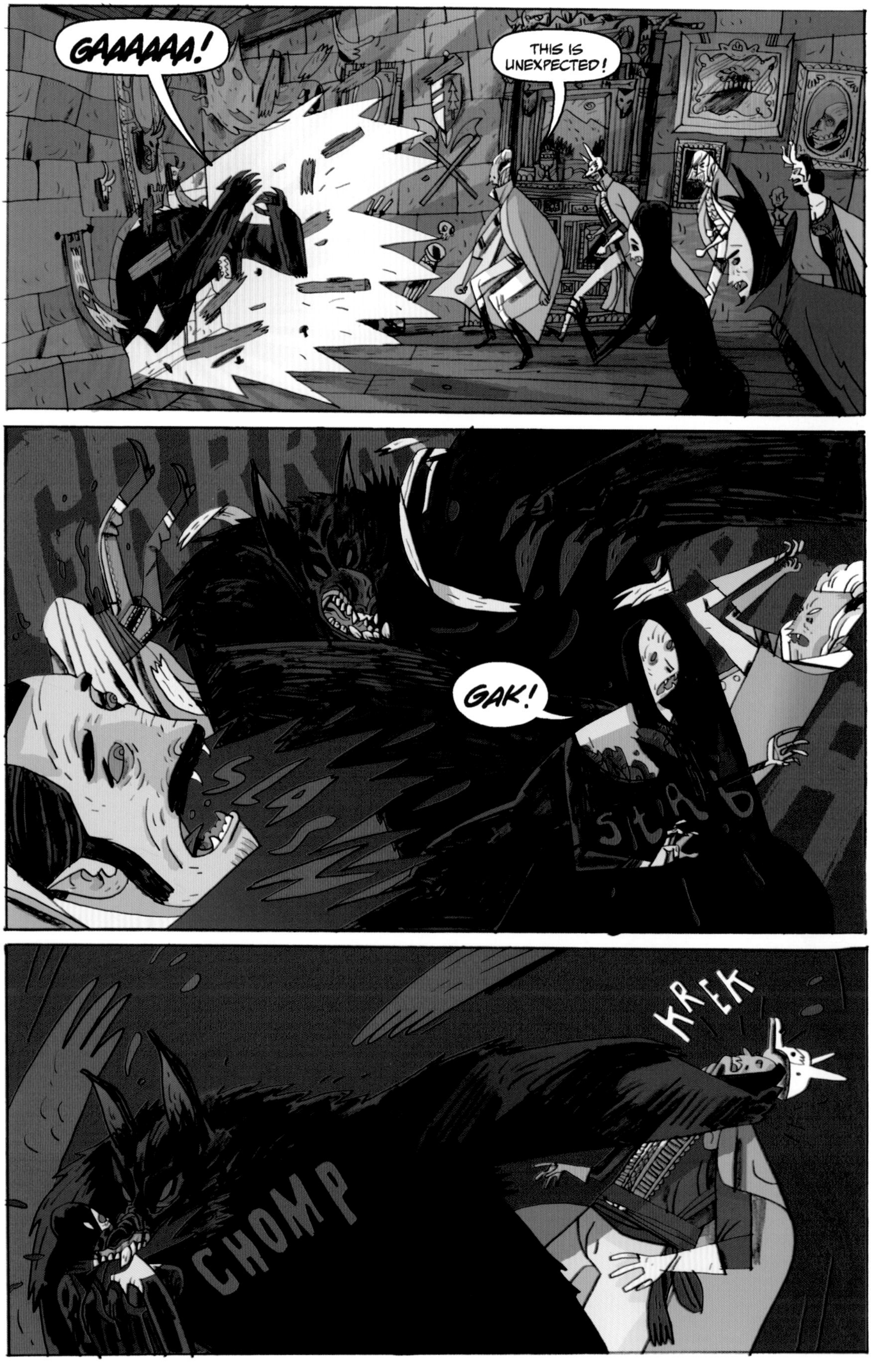
GAAAAAA!
THIS IS UNEXPECTED!
GAK!
SLASH
STAB
KREK
CHOMP

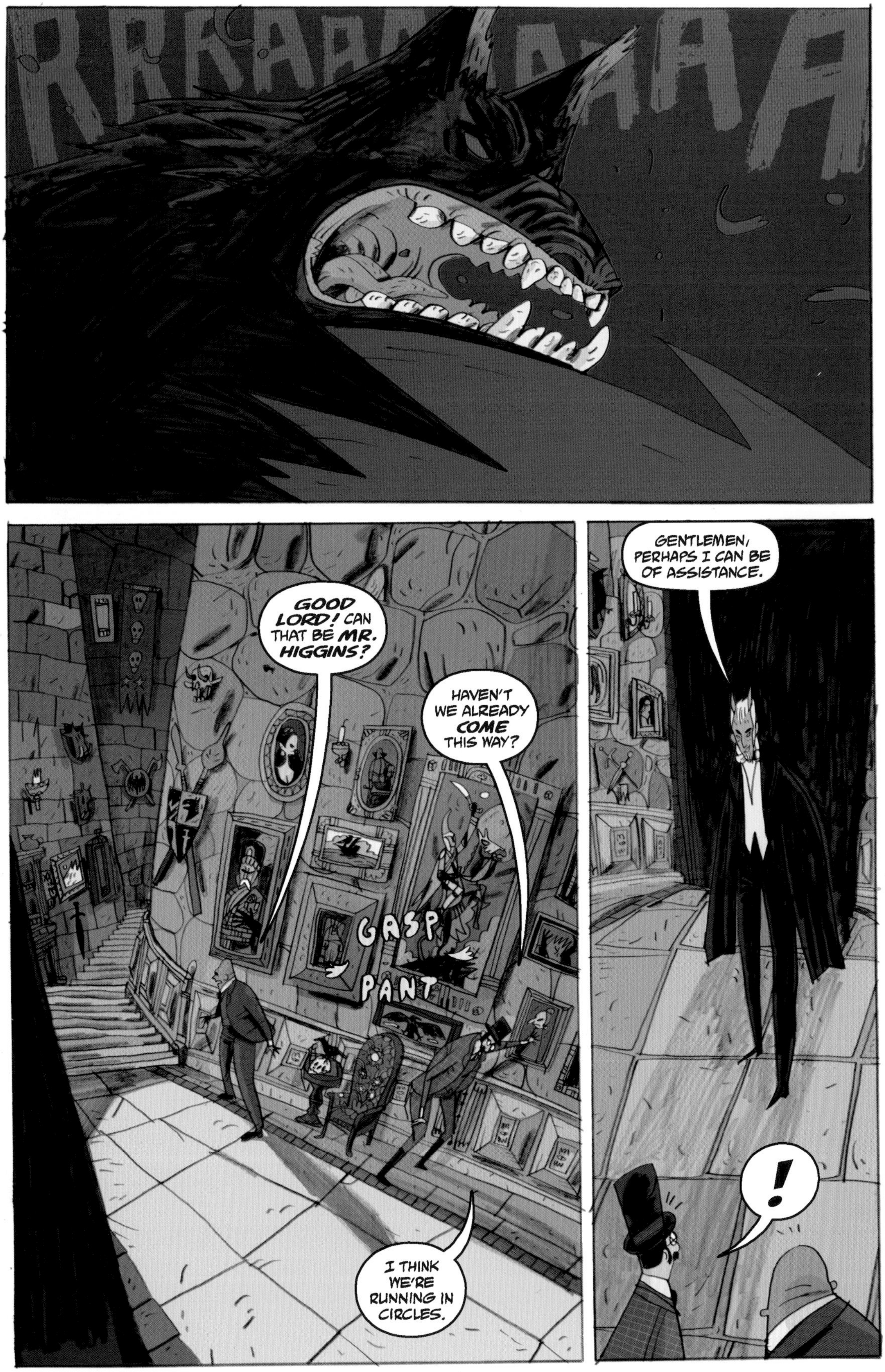
RRRAAAAAAA
GOOD LORD! CAN THAT BE MR. HIGGINS?
HAVEN'T WE ALREADY COME THIS WAY?
GASP
PANT
I THINK WE'RE RUNNING IN CIRCLES.
GENTLEMEN, PERHAPS I CAN BE OF ASSISTANCE.
!

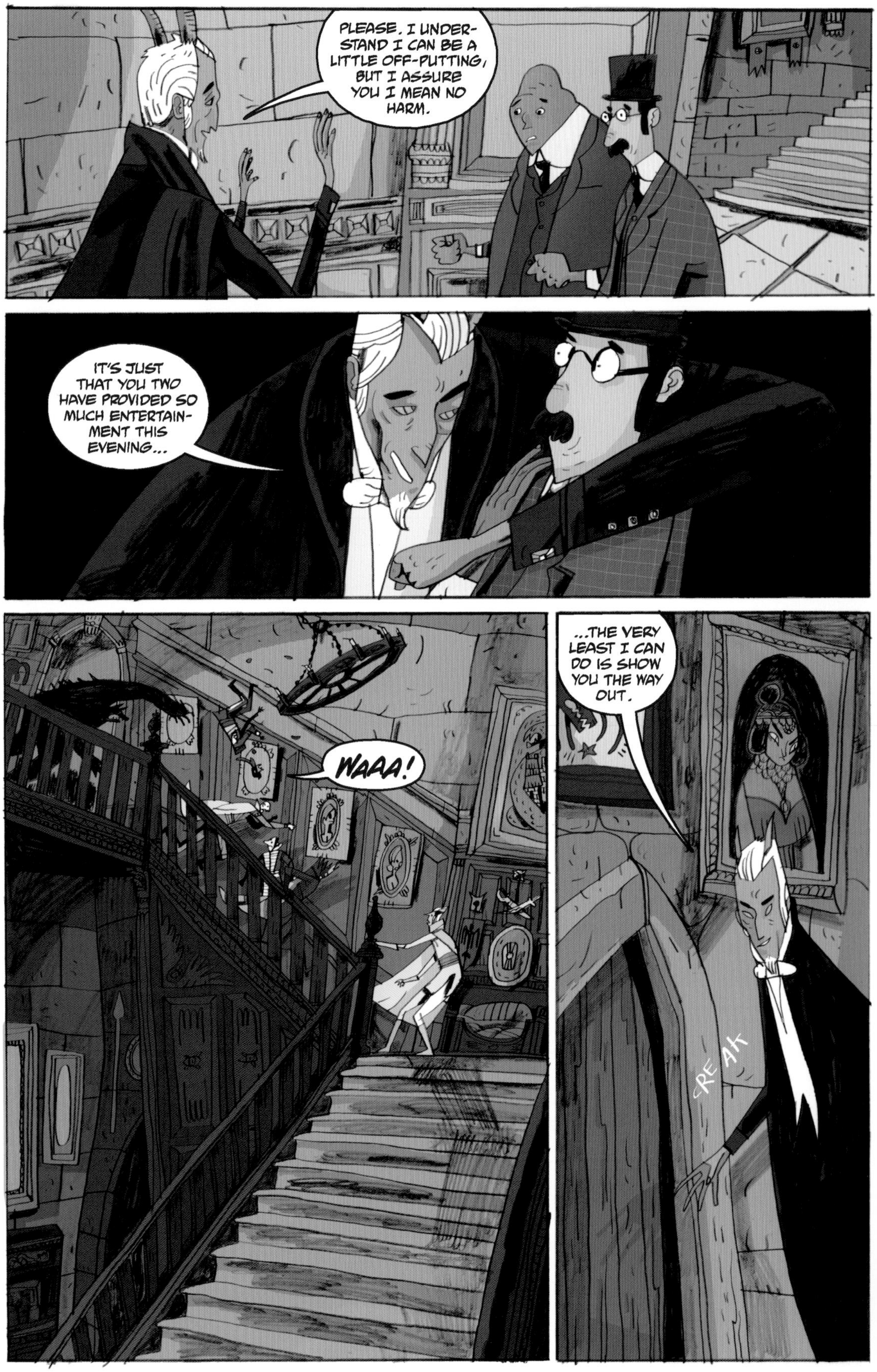
PLEASE. I UNDERSTAND I CAN BE A LITTLE OFF-PUTTING, BUT I ASSURE YOU I MEAN NO HARM.
IT'S JUST THAT YOU TWO HAVE PROVIDED SO MUCH ENTERTAINMENT THIS EVENING...
WAAA!
...THE VERY LEAST I CAN DO IS SHOW YOU THE WAY OUT.
CREAK

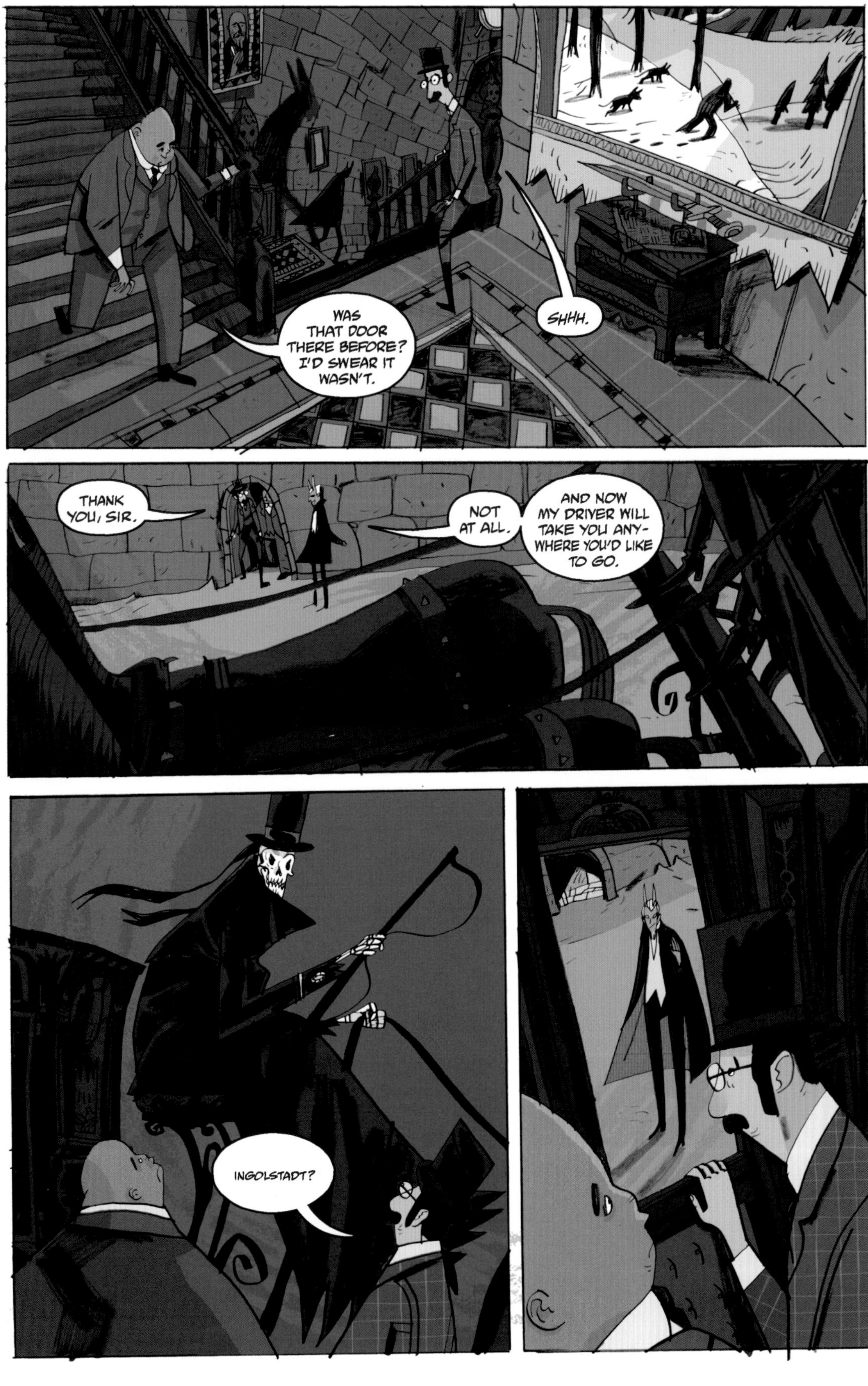
WAS THAT DOOR THERE BEFORE? I'D SWEAR IT WASN'T.
SHHH.
THANK YOU, SIR.
NOT AT ALL.
AND NOW MY DRIVER WILL TAKE YOU ANY-WHERE YOU'D LIKE TO GO.
INGOLSTADT?

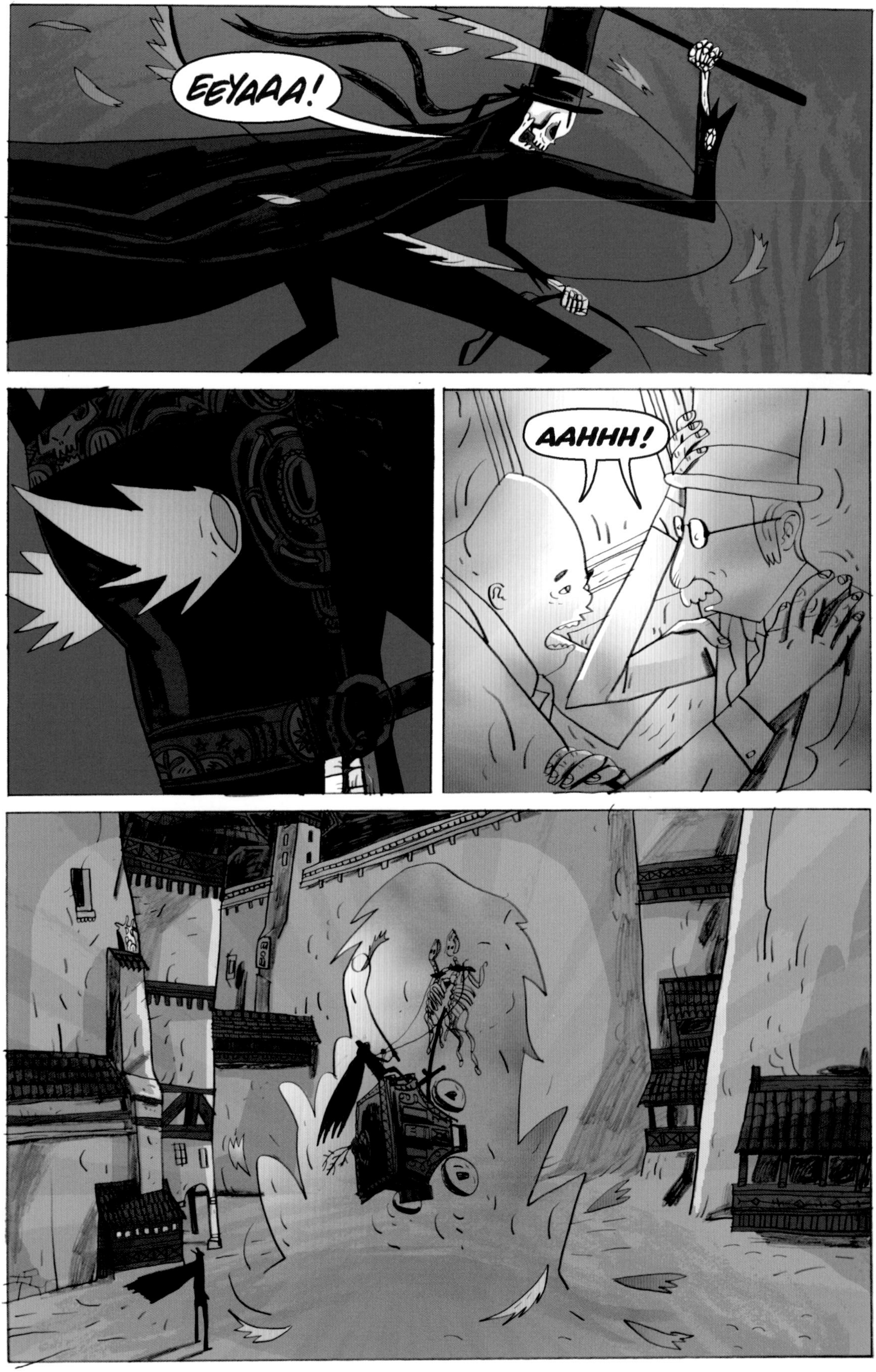
EEYAAA!
AAHHH!

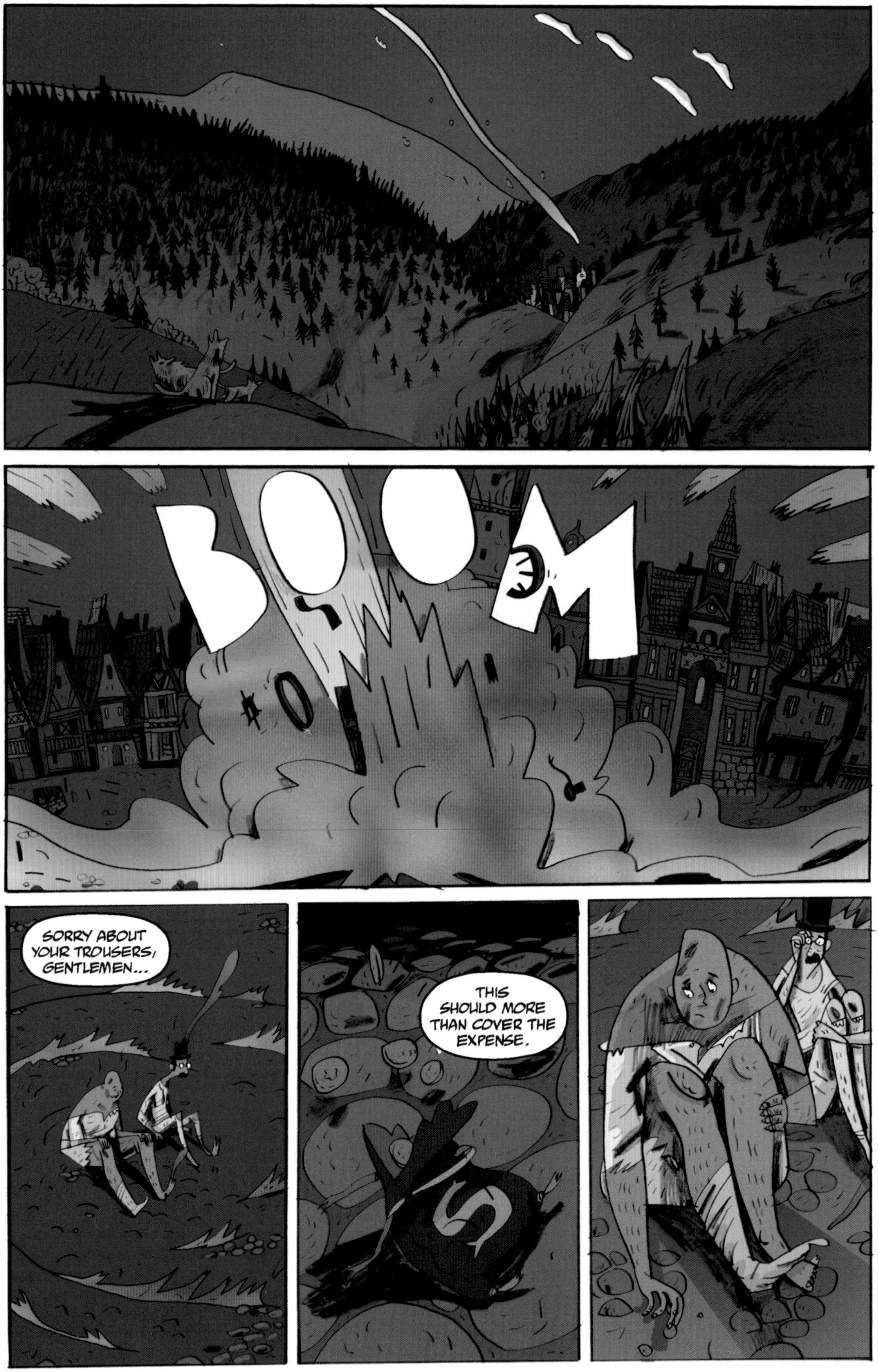
BOOM
SORRY ABOUT YOUR TROUSERS, GENTLEMEN...
THIS SHOULD MORE THAN COVER THE EXPENSE.

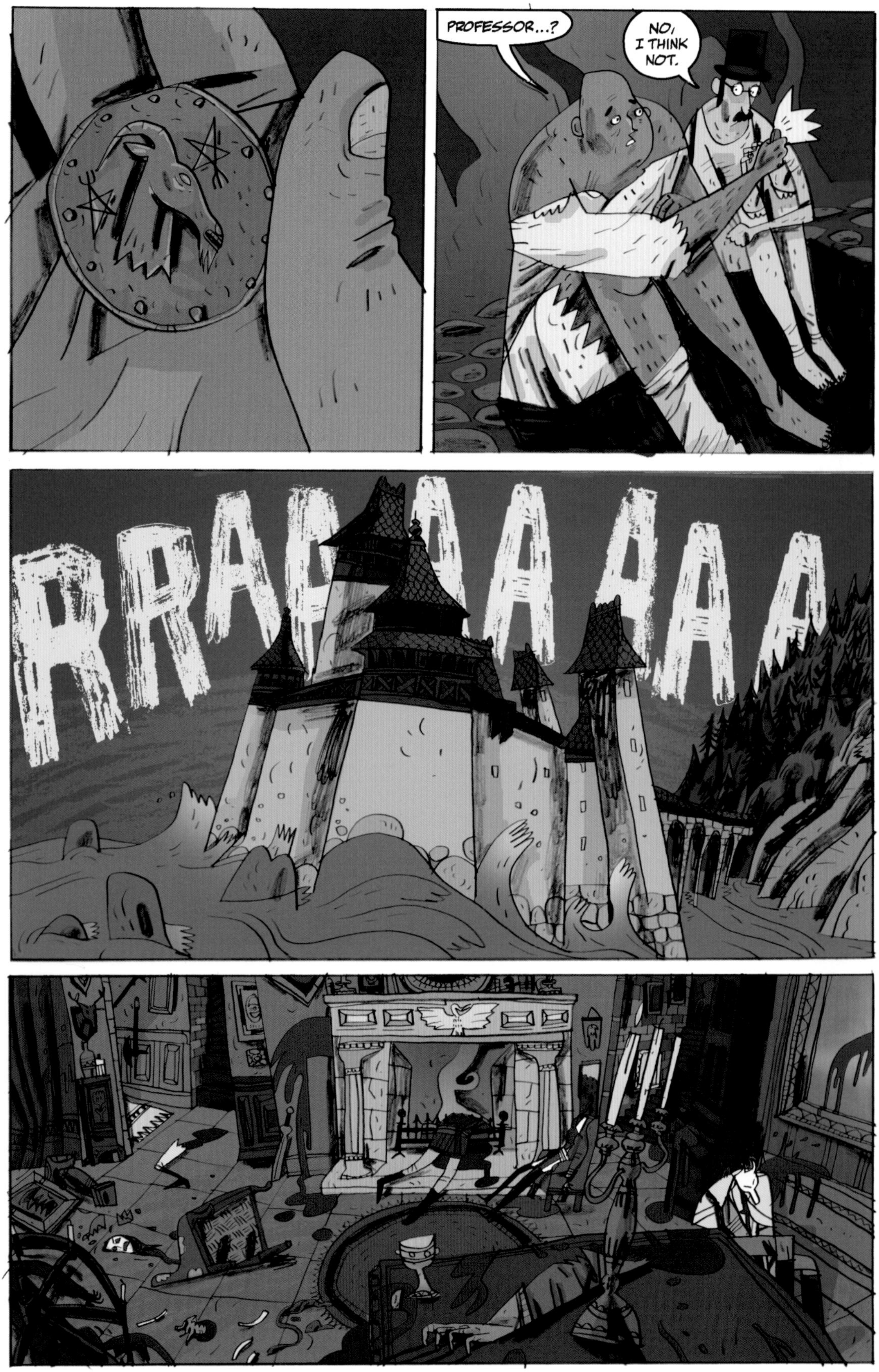
PROFESSOR...?
NO, I THINK NOT.
RRAAAAAAAA

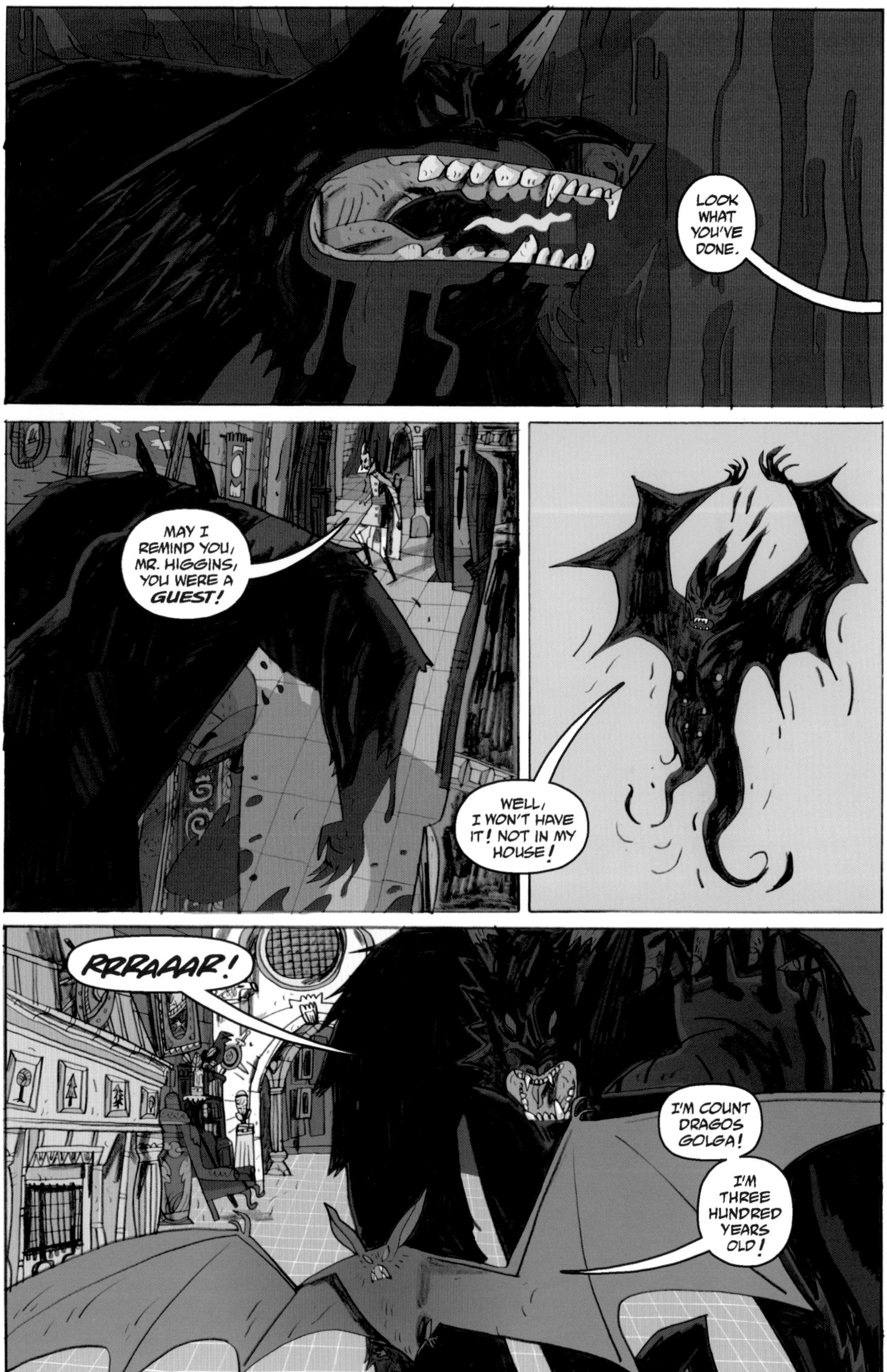
LOOK WHAT YOU'VE DONE.
MAY I REMIND YOU, MR. HIGGINS, YOU WERE A GUEST!
WELL, I WON'T HAVE IT! NOT IN MY HOUSE!
RRRAAAR!
I'M COUNT DRAGOS GOLGA!
I'M THREE HUNDRED YEARS OLD!

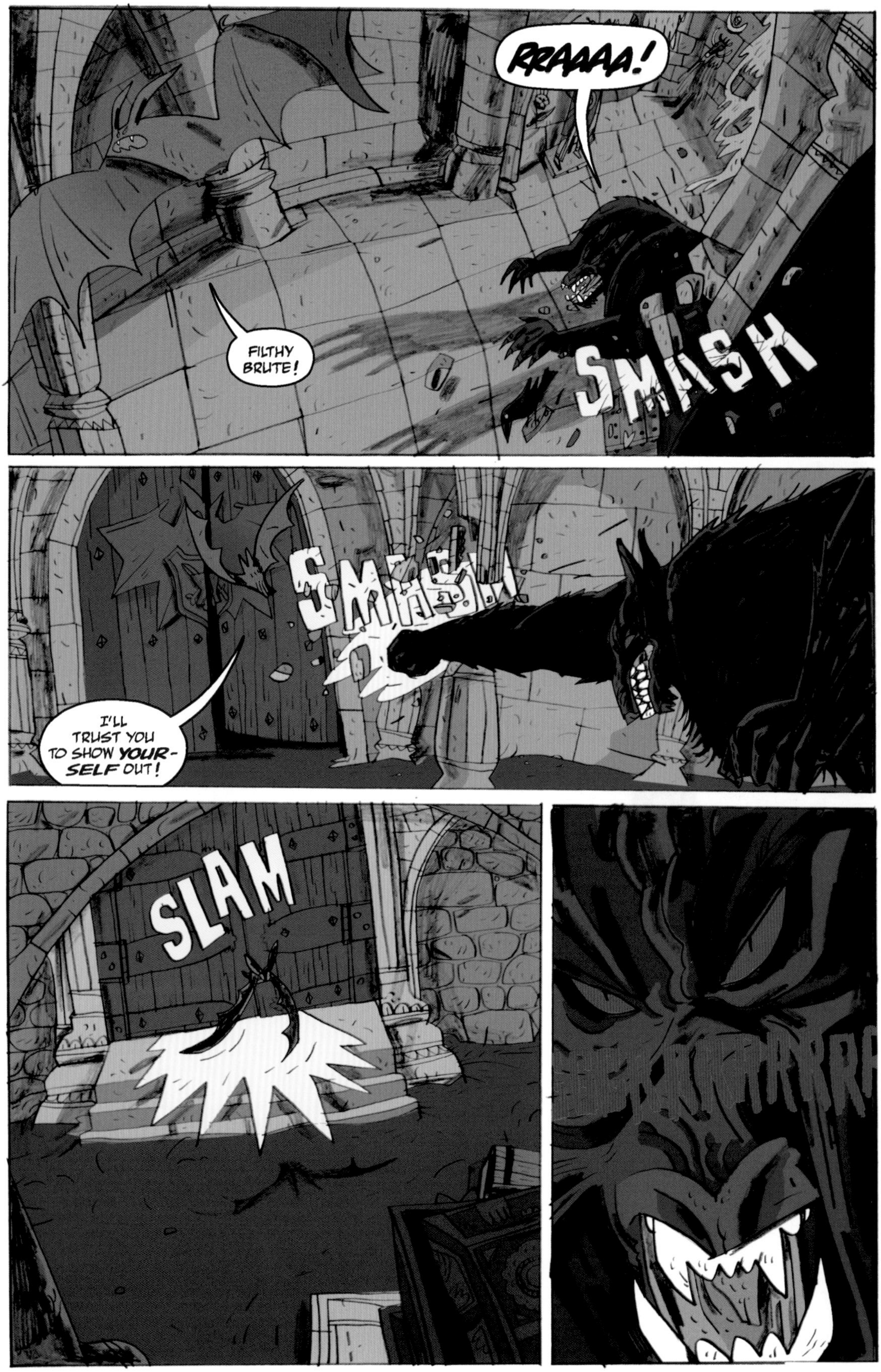
RRAAAAA!
FILTHY BRUTE!
SMASH
SMASH
I'LL TRUST YOU TO SHOW YOURSELF OUT!
SLAM

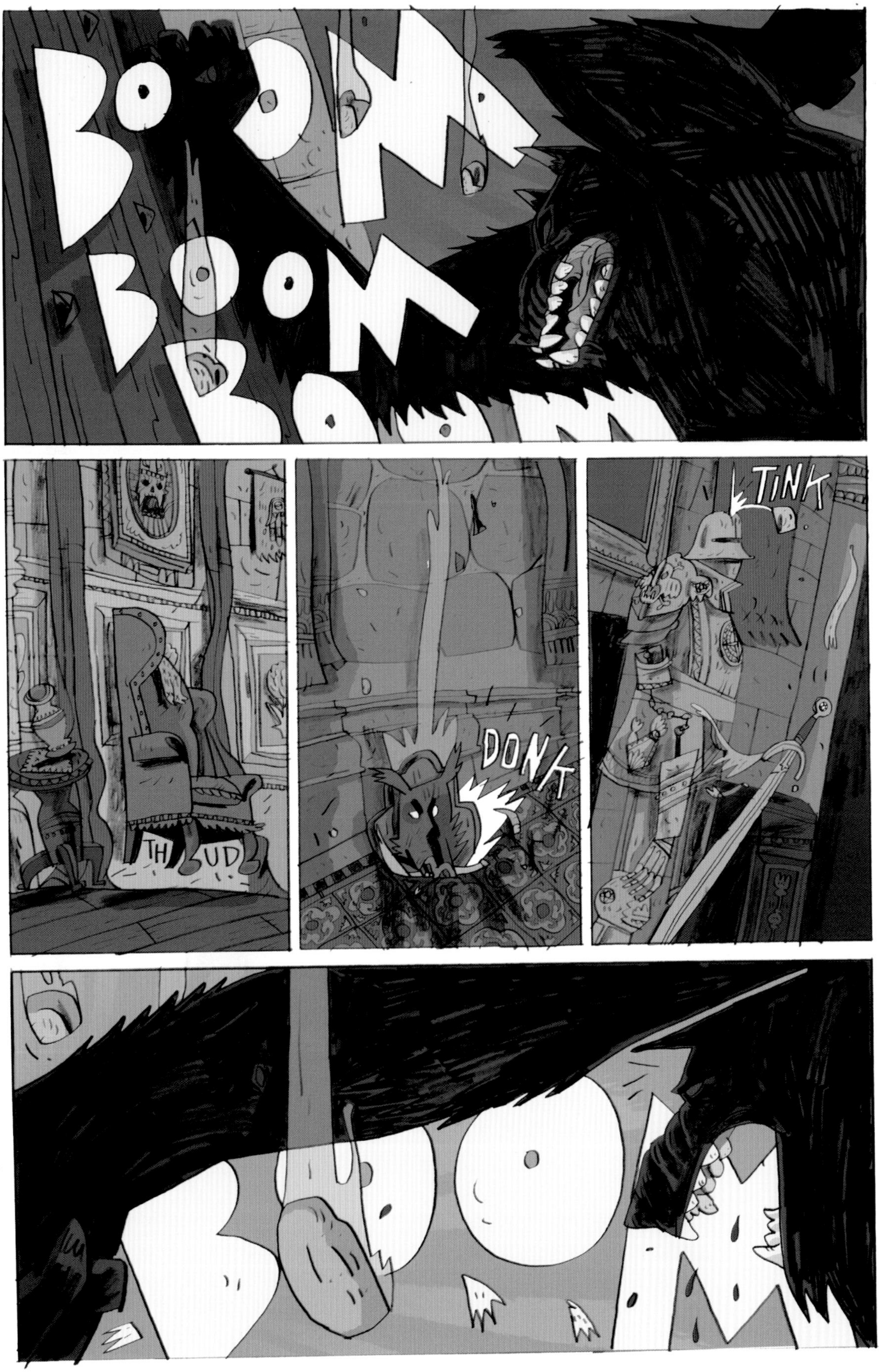
BOOM
BOOM
THUD
DONK
TINK

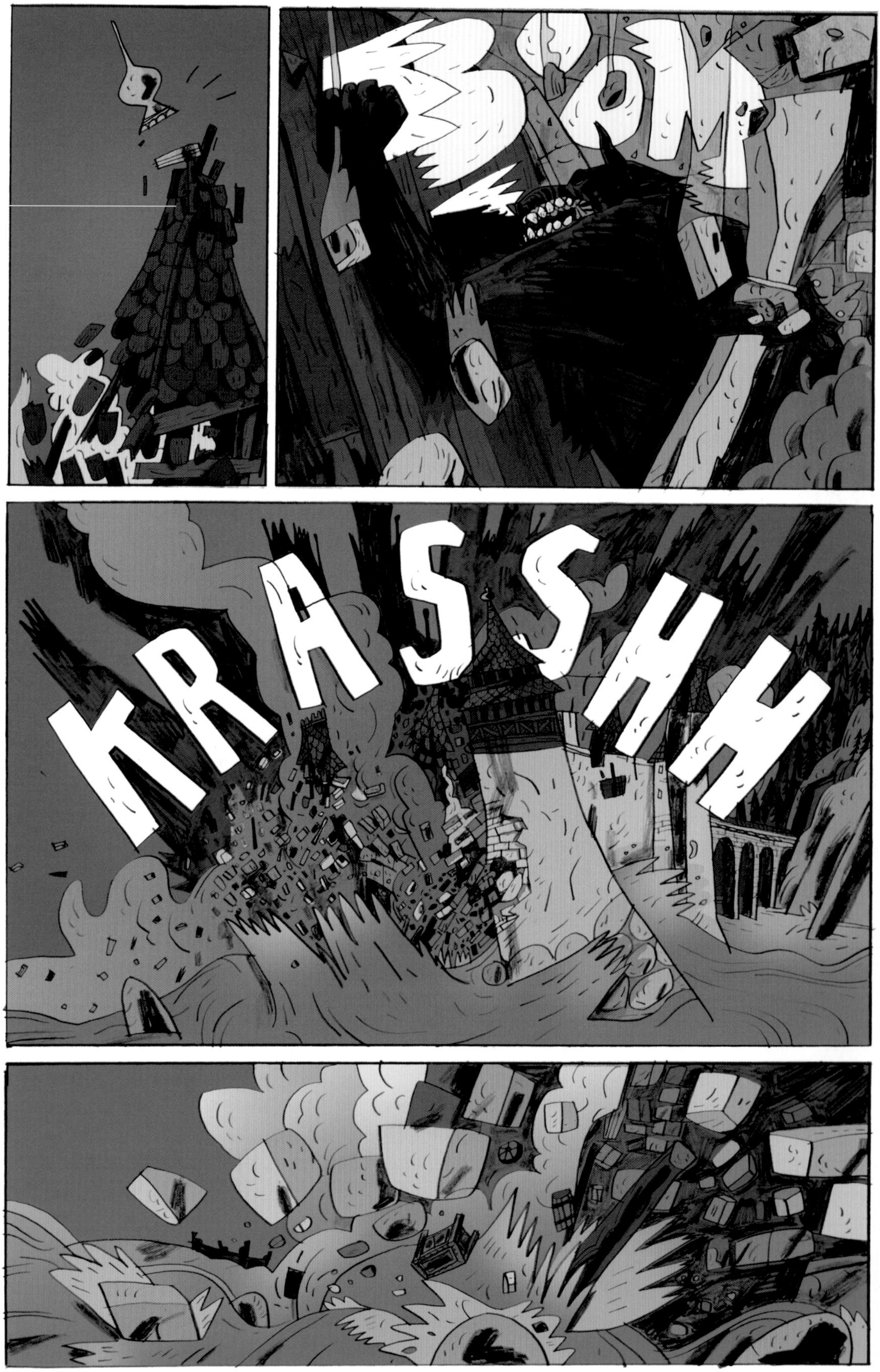
KRASSHH

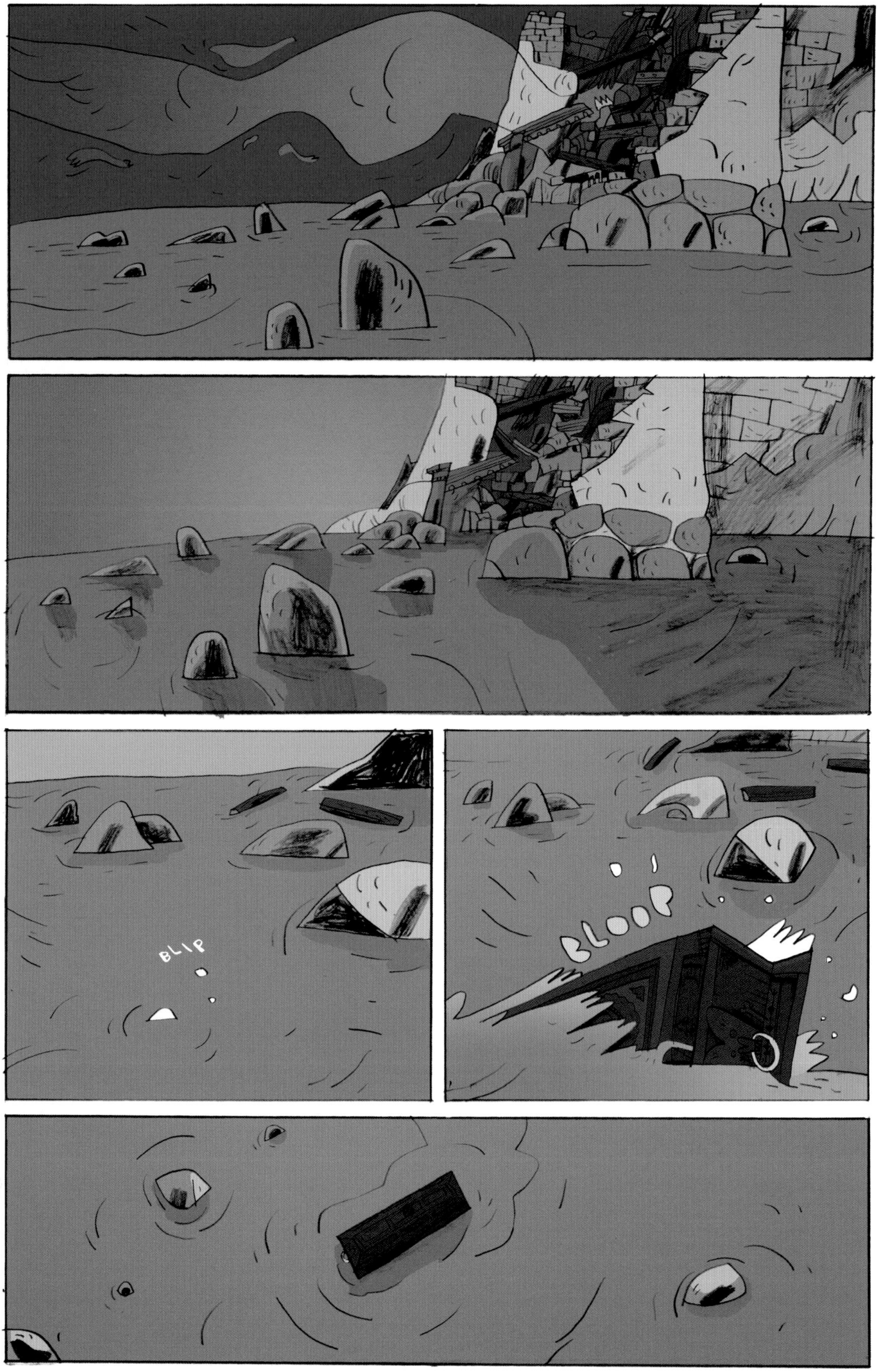
BLIP
BLOOP

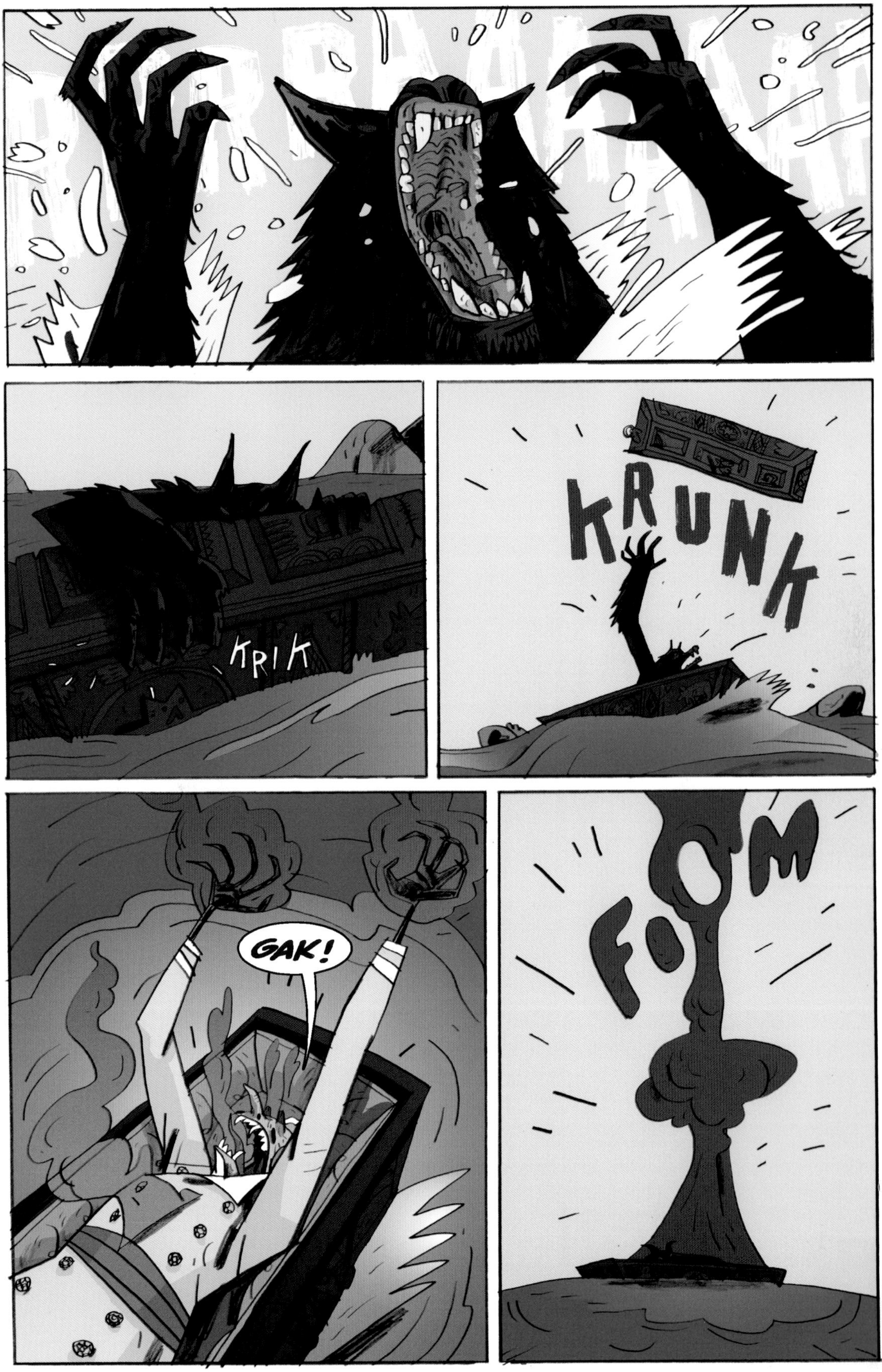
KRIK
KRUNK
GAK!
FOOM

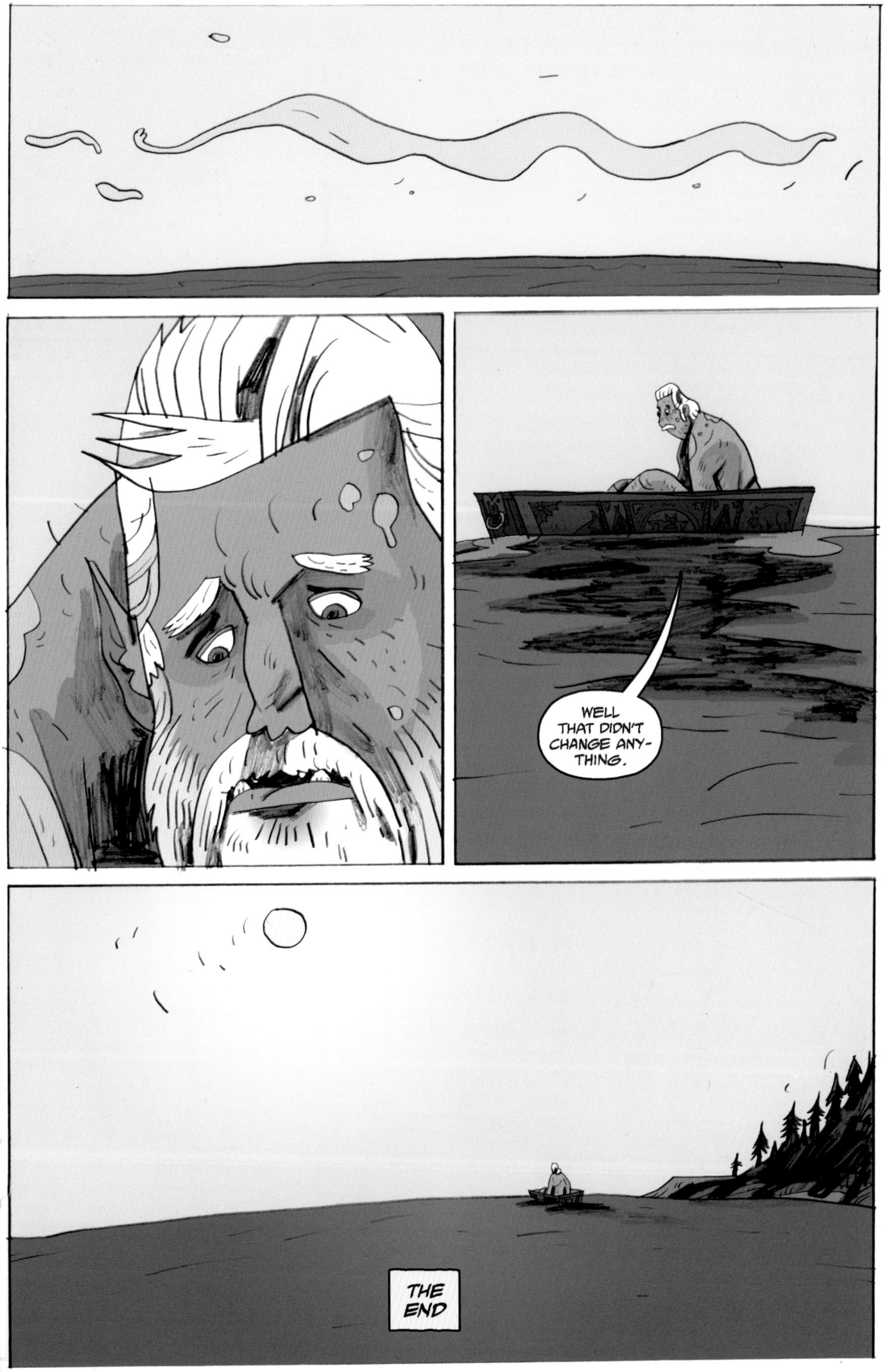
WELL THAT DIDN'T CHANGE ANY-THING.
THE END

RECOMMENDED READING

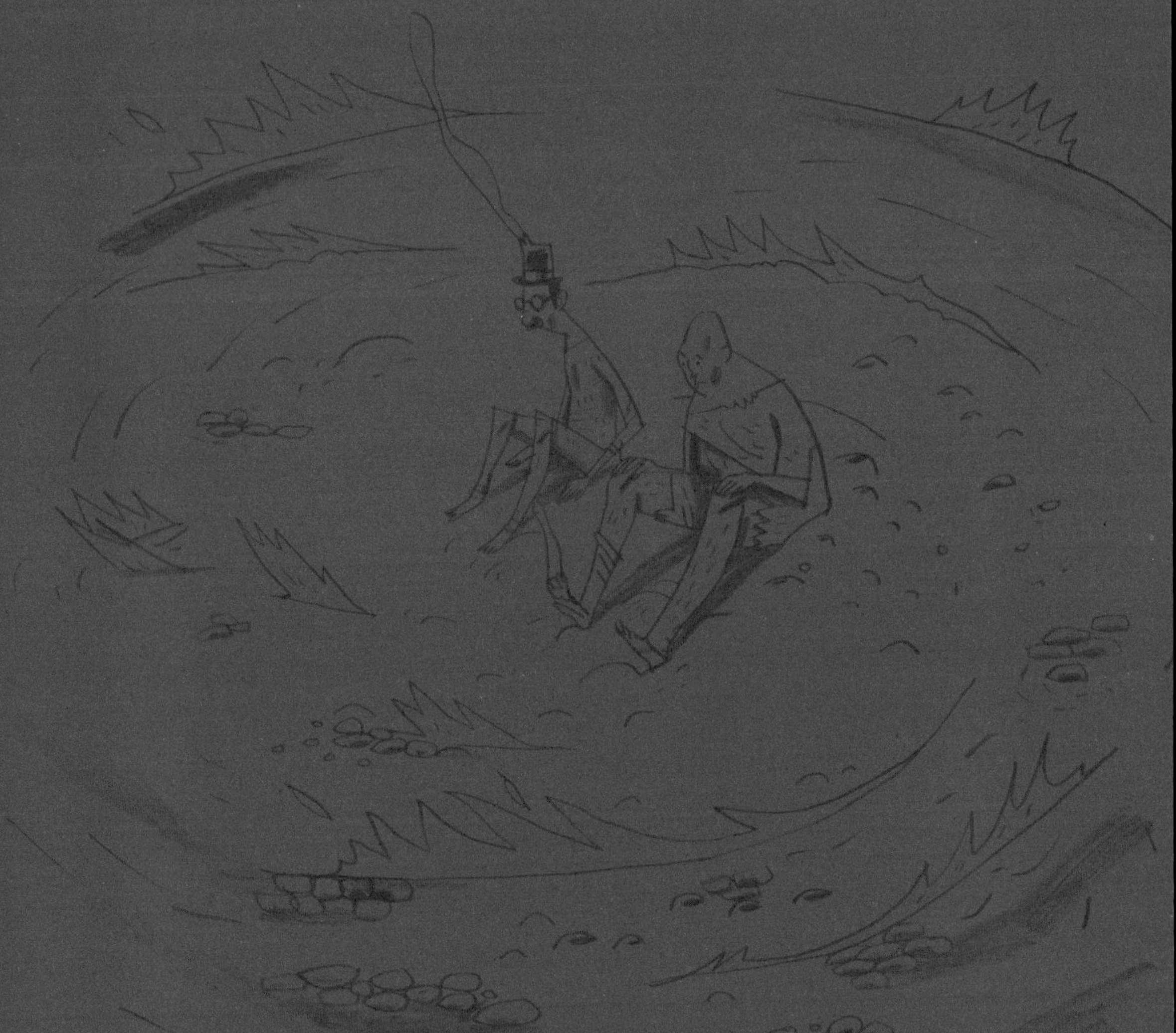

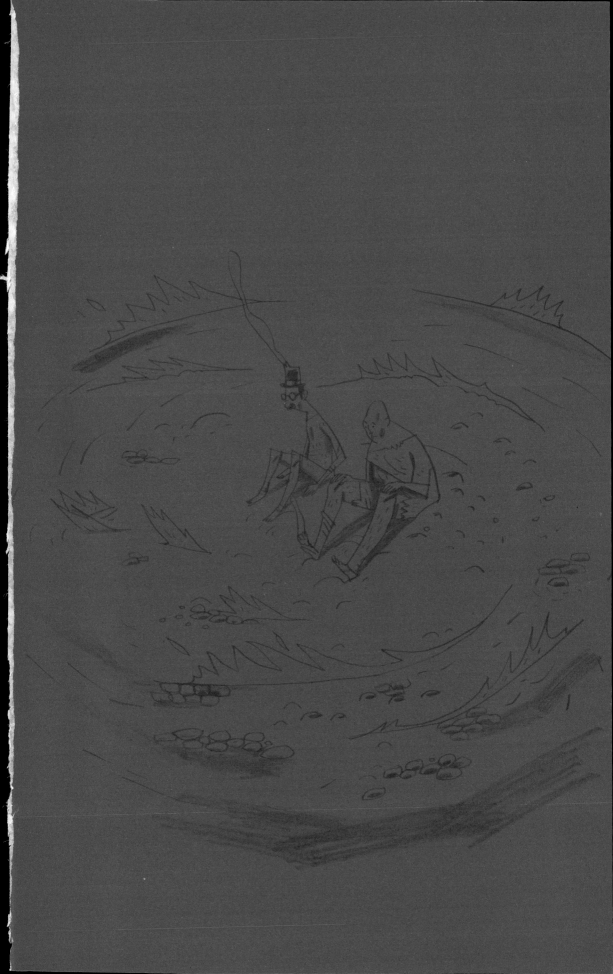

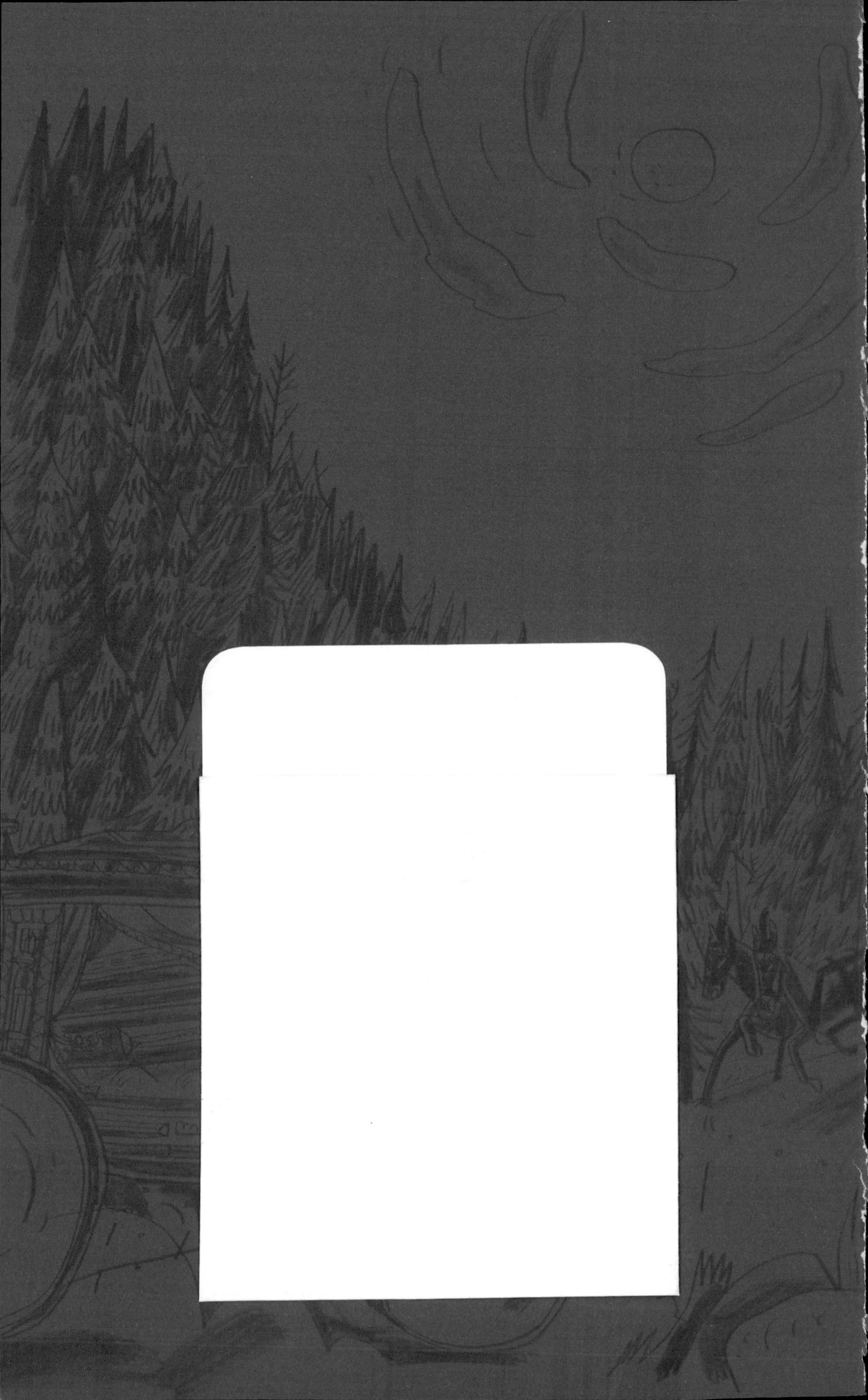